In a flash of agony, Adrea knew her Aunt Neadra was dead. Waking in hospital was strange enough, but having her colouring changed to that of her dead relative was a little hard to take.

Adrea called the authorities to let them know her aunt had been murdered and made the three-hour trip to get to her aunt's home.

Shockingly, things get out of control from there. She is arrested, questioned and released back to Ritual Space, where she has to seal the breach in the wards with her own blood.

Officer Hyl Luning is assigned to watch her, but he had better be quick, because she has an agenda that even she isn't sure of.

The characters and events in this book are fictitious. Any similarity to real persons, living or dead, is coincidental and not intended by the author.

Copyright © 2016 by Viola Grace
ISBN: 978-1-987969-21-4

©Cover Design Carmen Waters

All rights reserved. With the exception of review, the reproduction or utilization of this work in whole or in part in any form by electronic, mechanical or other means, now known or hereafter invented, is forbidden without the express permission of the publisher.

Published by Viola Grace

Look for me online at violagrace.com, amazon, kobo, B&N and other eBook sellers.

An Obsure Magic Book 4

by

Chapter One

Adrea worked to stock the shelves with the recently dried herbs that she had painstakingly prepared. The bell over the door chimed with perky insistence.

Adrea screwed a smile on her face and descended from the ladder. "Good morning, what can I get for you?"

When Adrea got a look at her client, she winced.

"It is that bad?" The woman's voice warbled from beneath skin turned toad green.

Adrea tilted her head. "Do you have any of the original substance?"

The woman reached into her purse. "I bought it near the old quarter."

Adrea opened it and sniffed, jerking her head back at the pungent odour. "Okay, that is an easy fix."

She gathered a bowl and got back on the ladder. With quick and economical movements, she gathered the ingredients for the salve that would restore the woman's skin.

Worts and weeds went into the bowl in quantities that she carefully measured after eight years of working in Foxes Tea and Herb Shop.

The bowl was polished wood, and scrubbing them out and oiling the work bowls was one of her evening duties. It was a neutral substance and would not alter the effects of the herbs.

When she had collected what she needed and returned to the counter, she picked up a glass pestle and ground the herbs into a fine powder.

"Does it smell?" Her client looked nervous.

"Like peppermint and chamomile." Adrea reached for some of the essential oils, and she mixed them in.

When the paste was mixed, Adrea grabbed a spoonful of the neutral face-cream base and mixed it all together before scraping every bit of the cream into a small screw-top container.

"That will be fifty dollars. Take it next door to Leda and give her the prescription."

The woman nodded eagerly and handed over the cash.

Adrea got her the change and slipped the small container into a paper bag before writing a prescription with the details of the ingredients. "Leda, next door to the left. Express Enchantments. She will have you out the door in a few minutes."

The woman nodded and clutched the bag to her chest as she nearly sprinted out the door.

Adrea shook her head and sighed. That was a rough one, but folks tended to get what they paid for in some of those old-quarter shops.

The bell rang again, and she looked up. She didn't need to ask; with a bit of flair, she measured out a series of herbs and set water to boil.

Ritual Space

The elderly woman took a seat in the teashop portion of the space and leaned over, "You are looking cheerful today, Adrea."

"I am always cheerful when you are here, Miss Crathmore."

"You know I have told you to call me Milly."

"I know." She winked. "And I have told you not to call me cheerful; it makes me look less than serious."

She poured the water into the pot containing her herb selection and set the pot and a teacup on a tray with a small container of honey and a spoon.

She carried the tea over to Miss Crathmore. Her high school teacher was looking spry for a woman in her nineties.

The tray was settled, and Adrea was heading back to the counter when agony ripped through her. She might have screamed, she tried to scream, but pinpoints of fire assaulted her body.

Miss Crathmore shouted, Adrea heard a phone being dialled and everything went dark.

The hospital was cold, sterile, and Adrea felt perfectly fine. She was laying in the bed, and to her less-than-impressed gaze, her parents were in the room.

Her father looked furious. "I can't believe that you did this, Adrea."

Her mother looked resigned. "You should have told us about this, Addy."

"About what? I had some kind of attack." She swung her legs out of the bed and got to her feet.

She wasn't even on any kind of IV.

Her mother reached to help her, but her father held his wife back. Adrea staggered past them and into the bathroom to wash her face. She leaned down, splashed cold water on her face, and then, she stood up to glare at herself.

She nearly fainted again. Her skin had lost all traces of a tan, her hair was snowy white instead of honey brown, and her eyes had gone from chocolate to vivid blue. She looked like her great aunt and namesake, Neadra. That could only mean one thing. Neadra was dead.

She wobbled back to the bed and sat down.

Her father scowled. "How long have you known about this, Adrea?"

"About what?"

"About you being Neadra's inheritor? The magic was supposed to come to me as her next of kin."

Adrea closed her eyes and took an inventory of her body. She felt miles away.

"Dad, the space can only be inherited by a woman. You know that."

He jolted. "You are lying."

A terrible sense of calm came over her. "I am telling the truth. Neadra told me that little tidbit when I was thirteen. I am surprised you didn't know, as you seem to be so sure of everything else."

Adrea looked at her parents and saw the small, ineffectual being who was her father, and the weasel that had birthed her. It was true enough that her mother was a ferret shifter, but looking at them through her new gaze, she could see the truth; they were grasping and greedy.

She went to the locker and grabbed her clothing, heading back to the bathroom and changing into her street clothing.

When she emerged with the hospital gown in her hand, a doctor was speaking with her parents.

"Doctor, I would appreciate it if you didn't share any of my medical information with them. They are leaving."

The physician blinked. "Oh, I thought they had your medical power of attorney."

She snorted. "Not likely. I am guessing that my boss called them. She is obsessed with healing the familial rift."

Her parents vibrated with indignation, but they had to keep themselves quiet with the doctor's ears perked to hear anything that would make them look less than credible.

"They are not on your next-of-kin list?"

"They might be, but I did not put them there. I live alone, and I plan to die that way. Now, is there any reason for me to remain in this facility?"

The doctor shook his head. "Aside from whatever magic altered your hair and eyes, you are completely normal. Better than normal, actually. Your medical results are perfect."

"Good. I will settle up with billing and get myself home."

She left her parents and the physician, and made her way to billing. Of course, the bill wouldn't be ready, but she couldn't stand another moment with her family.

Dorothea Minx was waiting for her, and she

dangled Adrea's purse from her fingers. "I have taken care of the bill, but I thought you might want your phone."

"You didn't have to do that, Doro."

"You passed out in my teashop. It is the least I can do."

Adrea smiled at her employer. "Sorry about that. There was a death in the family."

"Apparently you felt the shock." Doro looked her over. "It is a good look for you."

"It comes with a bit of baggage." She took her purse and slung the strap over her shoulder, digging for her phone. "Can you give me a ride back to the shop? I need my bike."

A glance at her phone told her that she had lost at least three hours.

"What are you doing?" Doro took her by the arm and led her toward the entryway.

"I am calling the Mage Guild. They are going to need to send someone to find Neadra's body."

She punched in the number for the non-emergency line and asked to be transferred to the Guild of Redbird City. She kept her voice calm as she described what she needed.

"My Aunt Neadra, proprietor of Ritual Space, has been murdered. I would like some of your officers to go to Ritual Space and examine the scene."

"Miss, how are you aware of this?"

"Ritual Space is a family inheritance, and I have now inherited the first wave of what is coming to me."

The officer sounded bored. "What would that

be, Miss?"

"I have inherited the magic."

She disconnected the call. All she could do was let them know and get her own ass to her aunt's home and business. The sooner her body was discovered, the better.

Chapter Two

She had been on the road for three hours when her phone started buzzing.

Adrea pulled to the side of the road, removed her helmet and answered her phone. "Hello?"

"Is this Adrea Morgan?"

"Morrigan. Yes."

"This is Officer Welling of the Redbird City Mage Guild. After a tip, we sent an officer to check on your Aunt Neadra, and I am afraid I have some bad news. Can you come to Redbird City?"

She snorted. "I am twenty minutes away from Ritual Space."

"Ah, I am still on scene. See you soon."

Adrea hung up and tucked her phone back in her bra. She started up her bike again, settled her helmet into place and drove to her aunt's home and the site of her demise.

Official vehicles crowded the parking lot near the expansive gates. The hole that they had hacked through the high fence told the story. No one had opened the gate, and they had not been able to enter using magical means. Sometimes, an axe was what was necessary.

She wove through the vehicles and parked next to the heavy and ancient oak and stone wall that kept the magic in and the uninvited out.

When she lifted her hands to remove her helmet, officers approached her.

"Miss, this is a crime scene. You can't be here."

She pulled the helmet free and shook out her hair. "I know. I called you. Adrea Morrigan of Ashfall City. I have driven for the last three and a half hours to get here. I am looking for Officer Welling."

Five of the nearest officers stared at her, and she smiled tightly. "Which way to Welling?"

The officer looking at her pointed toward the hole in the wall. She nodded, set her helmet down on her bike and walked through the wall and into Ritual Space.

Two mage officers were on the other side of the wall and muttering softly. Adrea frowned as she passed them, but then, she realized that they were holding back the stone. It was trying to seal itself again.

This was stupid. She needed to check in with Officer Welling and make her way to the centre of the property. Once she had done what she had seen Neadra do so many times, she would be able to control the doors.

Two men came by with a gurney, concealed by a white sheet.

"Miss Morrigan?"

She stopped staring at the body of her aunt as they took it away, and she turned to face the officer who had called her name.

The tall, blonde man paused in surprise when she turned. "Wow, that is uncanny."

"The hair colour is new. It happened this morning. The family resemblance of my features has been there all along."

He shook his head and extended his hand. "I am Officer Welling. Thank you for coming."

"The property was calling me, so I didn't really have a choice."

"If you will come with me, we will leave and I can escort you to our offices while we wait for the coroner to prepare your aunt for identification."

Adrea sighed. "I can identify her now. She has white hair, blue eyes and stab wounds here, here and here." She touched the places on her torso that had burned before she passed out.

She shook her head. "Oh, and I can't go with you yet. I have to go to the centre of the space and let it know that I am here."

"I am afraid that this entire area is a crime scene. You can't go anywhere." He went from friendly to stern.

She wanted to fight him, but she settled for asking. "Can I touch the outside of the wall?"

He frowned. "I don't see why not."

At least there was that. Neadra had referred to it as *locking the door*. If anything was trying to get out of Ritual Space, marking the wall with her blood should keep it in, even without the more involved ritual at the centre of the space.

They walked past the murmuring officers, and Welling spoke to them softly. She stepped through the hole a moment before they followed her, and when they were outside, the hole closed.

She turned away from the mages and walked down the wall, trailing her fingers along until she felt the slight snag into her skin that drew blood.

She whispered to the wall, "Keep tight against those who would use you or those who would escape."

A ripple went through the wall and moved outward until the stone appeared to buckle and reshape.

Welling ran up to her. "What did you do?"

She smiled and sucked her finger. "I locked the door. When you come back or need to investigate, bring me with you, and I will open it up."

"Miss Morrigan, you have just tampered with a crime scene. I am going to have to put you under arrest."

She glanced at her bike, and it glowed against the wall. It was protected.

"Fine." She turned her back, and he put her in cuffs.

Adrea looked at Ritual Space as long as she could. She settled back in her seat and watched as they drove past the fields of the countryside with the stretch of the wall on her left.

Near a copse of trees, she felt something unpleasant. The officer driving the vehicle shouted, and they swerved from side to side. Adrea saw the flash of green scales and one huge golden eye before they skidded to a halt.

She looked around, and there was no sign of the beast, but she could feel it out there.

She wasn't a mage and didn't even like magic,

but she could feel the pulse of the beast in the woods. "What the hell?"

"I am sorry, Miss. I don't know what that was."

Her driver got himself together and drove her to the Mage Guild headquarters, taking her by the arm as he helped her out of the SUV and down the sidewalk to the building.

Her hands were still cuffed behind her back, but the officer with her kept her upright. There was a surreal feeling to being taken into custody on the day that her aunt died.

It was so weird. She was operating completely on automatic. Her mind was scrabbling around trying to understand what was going on, but her body was sure of what it did and said.

Adrea heard herself say, "I need to speak with the commanding officer on duty."

"I need to book you in first."

"Trust me. Tell him that the inheritor of Ritual Space is here and I am not going anywhere until my lawyer arrives. It should be within the hour if he isn't here already."

They entered the sheltered hall, and she felt the passive wards pressing against her skin.

"You seem pretty sure that he is coming. I didn't see or hear you make a call."

"He would have been notified when my aunt died. From there, this would be his next stop."

The officer with her blinked, shackled her to a bench and went to speak to the desk sergeant. He glanced back at her several times, but when a familiar voice spoke from her left, she turned with a smile.

"Good afternoon, Mr. Grant."

The gargoyle with the suit and briefcase nodded. "Ms. Morrigan. You are all grown up; I am surprised you remember me."

She grinned. "You make an impression. I would shake your hand but..." she lifted her hands, and the cuffs clanked against the wood.

"Of course. I will get that taken care of right away. Your aunt left very strict instructions as to what I was to do for you. You will be set right in a few minutes."

Mr. Grant went to the desk sergeant, and the human straightened as the gargoyle rapped out information in no-nonsense tones.

A moment later, the sergeant was calling the captain.

When the captain emerged, he was the poster boy for the Mage Guild. Mr. Grant spoke quietly to him, and suddenly, an officer was undoing her handcuffs.

She got to her feet, and the captain ushered her and her lawyer into the offices.

Once she was seated with a glass of water in front of her, the captain gave her an embarrassed look. "Ms. Morrigan. I apologize for your arrest. The officers on the scene were not familiar with the restrictions of your property."

She inclined her head and sipped at the water. "It is fine, Captain."

"Linmoss. Captain Linmoss, Ms. Morrigan."

"Captain Linmoss. I want to know who killed my aunt."

He frowned and checked his report. "The preliminary report indicates it was suicide. Your aunt used a blade to cut her wrists."

Adrea's shock was a bolt of ice through her. "She didn't. She was stabbed three times in the torso. What did you say she cut herself with?"

He scowled, but Mr. Grant nodded. He slid the file over, and Adrea took a look.

She didn't have any history in law enforcement. She couldn't tell what was legal and what was medical, but she did know her aunt. "Impossible. That can't be the weapon if she was supposed to have killed herself."

The detailed icons on the hilt of the knife looked like they would fit right into Neadra's collection, but there was one little problem, it was steel. Neadra couldn't use steel as anything other than a paperweight.

She slid the file back to the captain and smiled tightly. "Neadra couldn't use steel. Nothing in her home was steel. Even her ornamental athame were made out of everything but steel. In her hands, steel wouldn't cut."

He frowned and looked like he was considering something. "How do you know that the killing blows were to the torso?"

"I felt them. The first one was to the left breast, the second just below and the third to the abdomen." She touched her body as she mentioned it.

He nodded and made a call. Whoever it was on the other end got the directions to make a complete search of Neadra Yoder for signs of magical or extranatural interference.

Mr. Grant smiled slightly. "Now, as my client is

the rightful owner of the property, she will take up residence immediately, allowing your officers to examine the grounds for clues as to who killed Madam Yoder. They will need to accompany her as the moment she introduces herself to the property, it will begin to alter itself to her nature in place of her aunt's."

The captain frowned. "Can't we delay the possession?"

Adrea nodded. "Sure. If you don't mind anything that can work a magic portal coming through the property and ripping through the weakened gates. My light connection with the walls is holding the power in check and keeping anyone from entering, but anything inside already could break right through the barrier. Ask the officers who brought us here. Something had already broken loose and is now scampering around the woods."

The captain was alarmed. "What is it?"

Adrea shrugged. "How would I know? My aunt had been dead for four hours or so by that point, and something large enough to freak the driver out is loose and running around. There is a lot of magic in there, and it wants to have an effect on the world."

Mr. Grant nodded. "My company has represented the owners of Ritual Space since this continent was settled. There can be no waiting in this case. She must get to the property as swiftly as possible to avoid any further leakage of magic into the surrounding area."

The captain rubbed his face. "You are right; it is

just so odd to be given an inheritance before the paperwork is ratified."

Mr. Grant grinned, showing fangs as steely grey as the rest of his body. "I have all the paperwork. That is what took me so long. If I didn't have to get the judges to sign the documents, I would have met Ms. Morrigan at the property. She was very quick."

Captain Linmoss nodded. "That brings me to a technical question. Ms. Morrigan, where were you six hours ago?"

"I was two hours into my shift at Foxes Tea and Herb Shop. I had just prepared a pot of tea for a customer, and then, the pain struck. Apparently, a few hours were wasted in hospital and then I was on my way here."

He nodded and made notes. "You had no idea that anything would happen? No premonition or any kind of magical notification?"

Adrea smirked. "I am not extranormal or extranatural. I have no magic. I want to study to be an herbalist, but as the shop owner said, it is better to leave magic to the magical. Even my aunt lived that way. She could allow doorways to Ritual Space, but she preferred folks to come through the gates."

Mr. Grant nodded. "Now, if you assemble your investigative team, they can meet us at the property. We will all go in together. As my client was definitely not at the property and has no magical abilities, she is not the killer you are looking for."

Adrea followed Mr. Grant's example and got to her feet. They left the Mage Guild's offices, and the lawyer held open the door of the passenger side of his customized vehicle. He tucked her in, closed the door and walked around to settle in the seat with a single narrow strut as the back. His wings moved gracefully to either side.

"I apologize for the wait, Ms. Morrigan. Judges are difficult to convince when the deceased person in question is of high station but low profile. They didn't want to just hand over the property. They didn't realize that all their secrets would be on display if they didn't."

She chuckled. "They realize it now?"

"Oh, yes. They will all be at the funeral. Neadra was a respected member of the community, even if few actually knew her."

He put the vehicle in gear, and they were on the way to what was about to become her new home. She just wished she knew what the hell she was doing.

Chapter Three

They sat in Mr. Grant's car for twenty minutes before the crime-scene team arrived.

Adrea got out, walked to the gate and noted that her bike was missing. She wasn't too worried about it; she had other things to focus on.

She ran her hands along the stone until she snagged her finger again. When the blood touched the rock, she smiled slightly and the main gate swung wide.

"Ladies and gentlemen, please be welcome in my home."

Adrea stepped into Ritual Space, and she felt surrounded by every blade of grass and each leaf on the property. They weren't minds or thoughts; it was simply a presence, a comforting sensation of familiarity.

She hadn't stayed over at Neadra's home in the last ten years, but before that moment fourteen years ago, she had spent every summer in Ritual Space.

Fourteen years ago, Neadra had taken her deep into the forest and drawn blood from her pinky, letting the soil taste her for the first time. It had also been the last time. Her father had forbidden her to return after that summer. It had had to wait until she had moved out, and then, she had to work for a living. The time to spend visiting her aunt had gotten shorter as she got older.

She shook herself out of her reverie as the team descended on the house and a few officers arrived to examine the surrounding space.

Mr. Grant touched her arm. "Ms. Morrigan, I have a few things for you to sign to make this formal. Where shall we..."

"Oh, the meditation house. There are tables inside, and it is nice and quiet."

He nodded and summoned one of the officers with a motion from his elegant grey hand. "We are adjourning to the meditation house; would you care to have someone clear it for us?"

The officer smiled slowly. "I will do it myself."

He moved gracefully, and to Adrea's eyes, it appeared that he didn't actually tread on the gravel. He moved so precisely that the stones didn't turn.

He was in plain clothes, so she guessed he was a detective, but she didn't know what the ranking system was in the Mage Guild.

It appeared that going through life blissfully ignorant was going to bite her in the ass. There were things in this world that she needed to know.

The man who was following the signs to the meditation house was a combination of at least nine different genetic donors. Her time in retail had taught her that much. He was a blend of all that was lovely and elegant and probably magical.

Mr. Grant's head came up, and his hooked nostrils flared. "There is blood."

The officer pulled two batons from holsters on his thighs, and he moved forward toward the door of the meditation house. The door refused to open for him. He thumped the lock, but his batons rebounded off.

Adrea stepped forward. "I can open it."

The officer marked an area. "Can you do it by touching here?"

She opened the tiny wound from earlier and tapped her pinky to the wood. The door shuddered and slowly opened.

She stepped back and remained on the deck alone while Mr. Grant took a look. He came out and put his hands on her shoulders. "You have found the primary crime scene. She was killed here and carried to her home."

Adrea swallowed. "Okay. Um, if you still wanted me to sign stuff, we can use the table overlooking the gardens. I doubt that it was compromised."

"Good, it is best that you not see this place."

She didn't need to see it. The bloodstains were marks of grief in the landscape. Her tenuous link to the property was already showing her things around her that she didn't want to see.

She numbly led the gargoyle back toward the main house and around back. As they left, she heard the officer use his phone to call the techs to come in and examine their actual crime scene.

Adrea didn't want to see it. She had known what had happened since the moment the knife struck.

Ritual Space

As they walked away from the building, her heart lightened. She walked around the house and to the back, entering the expansive gardens to the small table with two chairs in the centre.

The peace and tranquility of the gardens belied what had happened. Everything looked perfectly fine.

Mr. Grant sat and looked around. "I have never met with my client out here. It is definitely a different look for the space."

Adrea smiled tightly. "I only wish I could serve some tea. I think it would calm me."

"You are doing very well. Just hold on a little bit longer."

Adrea nodded. "Right. Well, what do I need to sign?"

The three inches of documents—some of which were even on parchment—were dropped between them. It was time to lose herself in paperwork.

Half an hour into the outlining of the banking structure for Ritual Space, a small squeaking came to her attention.

Adrea looked and grinned. "I had forgotten about them."

Four bunnies were drawing a tiny wagon toward her. There was a tea set and warmer on the wagon.

When they pulled up next to her, she lifted the set up and smiled. "Thank you. It is definitely appreciated."

The bunnies bowed and scampered off, leaving the wagon behind.

Mr. Grant blinked. "Do they normally do that?"

Adrea chuckled. "They are the remains of dozens of incomplete sacrifices. They eat herbs steeped in magic and have developed their own society. Neadra doesn't bother them, and they don't bother her."

She paused. "Didn't. Didn't bother them."

She busied herself with the tea, and while it was steeping, she signed the account cards for seventeen different banks. The amount of money that the property had accumulated was staggering. "What am I supposed to do with all of this?"

Mr. Grant smiled, showing his deadly teeth. "Whatever you wish. The funds of the renters of the space are accumulated in these accounts. They are now yours to do with as you will."

When the banking was complete, she looked at the next form and tears welled up. After Neadra's body was released, she had requested that it be interred in the private graveyard in Ritual Space.

She brushed the tears from her cheeks and signed the document. She would bring her aunt home to lie next to her family when the guild had finished its examination.

Mr. Grant offered her a handkerchief, and she blotted at her tears. "I am sorry."

"Don't be. It has been a lot to take in for you. Time moves slowly for my kind, and this amount of change would have caused my head to crack. You are holding up very well."

She chuckled softly. "Thanks. I am trying. There is an odd feeling inside me, like something is trying to get out."

"That is the property. You are linked to the wall, but you haven't taken control of the land itself. You will need to take care of that, but I am guessing that you are aware of it."

She nodded. "As soon as I do, the house will change. I have to hold off as long as I can so that they can examine everything."

"You are doing very well. When Neadra came to me and made these arrangements, I had my doubts that you would be a suitable replacement. Now, I am not so sure I was correct. You seem to have an inner strength that I was unaware of. You will do well in your new home."

Adrea smiled slightly. "Thanks for that. I will launder this, and get it back to you."

"Keep it. I always bring a few when wills are in the offing. There will still be an official reading of the will on the day of the funeral, but we have handled the portion that involves the corporation of Ritual Space."

She exhaled, and he tucked the paperwork away.

"I will provide you with your copies on the day of the funeral. I will also handle the arrangements in the manner your aunt desired."

Adrea quirked her lips. "You do know she wasn't really my aunt."

"Great aunt twice removed. Her lifespan was far longer than she admitted, but that is the bonus to this place. Your life mixes with the land and your body given its power of renewal. You can't go far from it, but it will keep you alive and healthy."

"Once I complete the ritual."

"Indeed."

She sighed and picked up her teacup, getting to her feet to look out at the gardens. "This was always my favourite part of the grounds."

She looked around, and if she focused on the slight movements, she could see the rabbits tending the plants. Adrea took a few steps toward the wild roses, and she spun as if struck.

Pain ripped through her shoulder, and she went down on one knee.

"Ms. Morrigan, what is it?"

"Something else just hit the wall. It is trying to get out."

Mr. Grant got to his feet. "I think that now is a good time for you to complete your link to the property."

She gritted her teeth as the pain moved across her back. "Are they done with the crime-scene stuff?"

"It doesn't matter. You must do this or the gates will start to feel pressure and you will be torn apart."

Adrea grunted as the pain continued to travel, seeking a means of escape. "I think you are right. Please let them know to get moving."

She stood up, set her teacup down and ran through the gardens, into the forest.

She was running to find the centre with someone trying to punch their way out of her skin. Thank goodness she was wearing the right clothing for the job. There was nothing worse than being overdressed when you opened your mind and body to join with a few hundred acres of land.

Chapter Four

The centre was surprisingly subtle. A light growth of new trees in a circle and lush green grass in the centre.

As she passed the circle, she could feel something weird. Those trees were hers. They looked to be about six months old, but those trees were hers.

Sighing, she knelt in the centre of the ring and clawed at the ground. She had heard Neadra say dozens of times, *the earth provides for us,* and as she dug and tiny shards of stone pricked her hands, she finally understood.

She kept digging until she found a wide blue stone, the same colour as her eyes. Tiny smears of her blood covered the stone.

Adrea lay on her belly and breathed into the hole she had dug. She whispered the words that Neadra had said in front of her. "I trust you, I guard you, I watch those who walk your path. Bound by body, bound by blood."

She repeated it over and over as the light began to flicker in the blue stone. She pressed her hands to it and kept chanting as the power built to a crescendo and bright blue light cascaded over her, flowing outward from the centre.

Adrea breathed in the green around her, felt the stone in her bones, the soil under her skin and the grass in her hair. She inhaled and exhaled in a slow rhythm as the wave moved outward until the wall was encompassed and she was complete.

She knew every inch of the property like she knew herself.

Relaxed and confident that she could subdue anything that tried to break out or in, she covered her digging site and got to her feet. A sprout shot up through the ground and rapidly turned into a young oak.

Her mark on the property was sealed with that oak.

Adrea Morrigan straightened her shoulders and went to find the intruders in her territory. Eleven mages, one gargoyle and a half-elf were in her space. She was going to meet and greet every one.

She walked with a determined air and headed through the woods and back to where Mr. Grant was still going over his paperwork.

"So, Ms. Morrigan. Did you catch the creature you were after?"

"No, but I now know where it is, and I will subdue it if it becomes a problem."

He gave her a respectful nod. "Neadra told me that you were perfect to be her successor. I am beginning to think she was right. You are definitely up to this challenge."

"I do hope so, because Ritual Space is now

mine."

"Excellent. There is one more thing. Neadra provided you with this starter's manual. It will tell you how to proceed in the business of providing magical property for temporary use."

He hauled a heavy book out of his bag and placed it on the table in front of her. The manual was huge, at least a foot square and encrusted with gems, petrified wood and bits of freshly mined metals. When Adrea opened the book, each page held a pressed flower or leaf.

Without asking, she knew that everything in that book had come from the property around her.

Mr. Grant scowled. "I am sorry. She said she had written it for you."

Adrea looked at the page and smiled. Her name was written on the paper with the distinctive flourish of her aunt's hand. "She did. Don't worry. I will get by."

He nodded but appeared confused. "If you need me, here is my card. I will contact you when the details for the funeral have been completed."

"Thank you."

"The ceremony, burial and reception will be held here. You can expect about seven hundred guests. Do not worry. The function will be fully catered. They are coming to pay their respects to your aunt and to greet you."

Adrea blinked. "Seven hundred?"

"Yes, you will have to open the gateways to allow them to come, but many will respect your recent acquisition of the property and lack of training and car pool, so to speak."

She smiled weakly. "Oh, good. I am glad I have a few days to get the hang of that."

Mr. Grant patted her on the shoulder. "As Neadra always said, it is in the blood. I am sure you will do just fine."

She nodded. "Right. Any idea where I am supposed to stay?"

"The house will provide for you. I am guessing that it is your motorcycle on the inside of the gate?"

She blinked. "I didn't think to check. I am guessing yes."

"Then, you have a way to obtain what you need meal wise, though the garden is usually fully stocked."

Adrea chuckled at his tone.

"I think I might just head out and find some takeout."

"If the property lets you out, feel free. If not..." He took out a notepad and jotted down a number. "This is the name of a Chinese restaurant that will deliver out to this place."

"What do you mean if the property lets me out?"

"You are currently in the process of bonding to this land. It will become part of you and you part of it, but this takes time. Neadra said it took weeks. Be prepared to fend for yourself and send me lists of anything you need. I will have my assistant bring it to you."

She blinked rapidly. "Oh. Right. Gotcha. I think I need time to plow through this book anyway."

She thought about it, and despite the length of

time since her last stop on her bike, she wasn't hungry. She would wait until hunger stirred before worrying about where food would come from. She had other things to focus on.

Adrea closed her eyes and found one remaining mage. He was standing outside the house and guarding it. She guessed he was guarding it; he wasn't moving.

She walked Mr. Grant out, and he left her behind. The door closed and locked behind him, so she turned and went in search of the final officer.

She found him standing in front of the house. "Excuse me. Everybody else has left."

He nodded. "I am aware. I received a call that outlined your importance. You have been assigned a guard around the clock until we know you are capable of managing your own defense."

She frowned. "That sounds annoying. What is your name?"

"Detective Luning."

Adrea twisted her lips. "Do you have a first name?"

"Hyl. It's a family name, Ms. Morrigan."

"Call me Adrea. My aunt never stood on ceremony, so neither shall I."

He smiled. "Adrea then. Are you ready to enter your home? You were right, by the way. The house began to make itself over the moment that the energy wave struck it. Without your warning, our teams would never have gathered what they did."

She swallowed and looked at her aunt's home, but it wasn't her aunt's home anymore. It was changing shape to alter itself into the long Victorian style that Adrea favoured. It was very charming. Now, it was time to find out what happened to Neadra's collections.

The crime-scene tape was dangling from the doorway. Detective Luning pulled it away, and he tried to open the door.

Adrea chuckled and pushed him away. "My door, my chance to open it."

She pressed the lever and pushed the door open, swinging it inward. The dark wood floors and open structure proved that the house was hers. It was everything that she wanted in a home; she just hated how she had come to have it.

"The crime-scene team took pictures of everything, which is a good thing as this place is completely transformed. I have never seen anything like it before."

"You haven't been here before?"

He shook his head. "No. I have only recently transferred to Redbird City."

"Where did you transfer from?"

Detective Luning didn't answer. He responded by saying, "I will clear the building and guard the door."

"Good luck with that. The doors in here won't open for you."

He frowned. "Why not?"

"Because I have to key each room to my preferences. Tell it what I want it to be. This was originally a haunted house; a house of refuge hosting a welcoming spirit. Now, it houses the manager of Ritual Space."

The book in her arms warmed, and she really

wanted to read the message from her aunt. "Well, you can do what you like, I am going to sit in the kitchen and read."

"I will check the kitchen before you settle."

Adrea looked at him, and he seemed puzzled by his own insistence. "Seriously. You can go."

He shook his head. "There is something here. Something watching you. I can feel it."

She closed her eyes and opened them when she had identified what he was sensing. "Oh, that is just the rabbits."

"Rabbits?"

"People come here to cast spells without them getting loose. Those who want reproductive spells generally start with rabbits. Many of those folks don't have the heart to kill them, which leaves bunnies running loose on the grounds. They absorb a bit of magic over time, and as I am the guardian of the property, it is in their best interests to keep an eye on me. As long as I am healthy, no predators walk these lands."

"Rabbits?"

She laughed and gestured for him to follow her through the house. She walked across hardwood and looked at the pale marble that now made up her home.

Detective Luning murmured, "No metal. Plastic but not metal."

Adrea didn't comment on his perception. He was right. Neadra couldn't use metal, so there was no reason for it to be in her house.

The door at the back of the house opened on the herb garden. She listened to the crunch of gravel under her feet, and he followed her, a silent shadow at odds with the very cheerful clumps of plants.

"Guys, please come out and introduce yourselves to Detective Luning. He doesn't believe you are here."

The herbs rustled, and a large grey rabbit emerged. More rustling and a bunny in white, another in brown and then dozens more gathered on the gravel.

Adrea knelt and held out her hand. "Blueberry!"

The white bunny with the deep blue stripe between his ears hopped up to her and jumped into her arms.

She snuggled with the beast that should have been long dead. Blueberry was a decade if he was a day. Bunny rabbits just didn't live that long.

The quivering ears and twitching noses of the other rabbits were all focused on Luning.

"He's fine, guys. It is nice to see you again. Thanks for the tea earlier."

The rabbits hopped up to her, one by one, and touched their heads to her knees. It was a ceremony. The rabbits depended on the land and that meant they were dependent on her. They were swearing fealty to her in their own fuzzy way.

She continued to cuddle Blueberry until the last of the bunnies had paid homage.

"With this many adults, I would think there would be more babies." Luning crouched next to her.

"Nothing gives birth here. This isn't a place for

the future; it is an eternal present. Time does not march on here; it simply holds itself still as the world moves around it." She smiled and set her favourite bunny down. He hopped off with the rest of his herd.

"Well, Detective. Was this what you sensed watching me?"

He scowled and stood up. "Part of it. There is more."

"Well, you can keep an eye out for my stalkers and I will get my studying done." She rose to her feet and swayed a little.

He caught her with an arm to the middle of her back, and she hoped that the dimming light covered her blush. She turned and bustled back into the house, leaving him to trail behind her.

She was relieved to find that she had not put the book down while cuddling with her buddy.

Adrea sat at the kitchen table and started to read. It was time to find out what she was in for before she started working on who killed Neadra. That was what she would do in the morning.

# Chapter Five

The elegant handwriting laid it all out for her in a few sentences.

Dear Adrea,
If you are reading this, I have met my end. You are now the manager of Ritual Space, and there are a few things you need to know.
One, I am sorry, but the life you knew is over. Your life has joined to the land, and it will keep you close until that bond is strong enough to stretch a little. That should come in a few months, until then, the back of this book has a number of nearby businesses that will deliver to you.
Two, you don't need to renew your link to the land every year. Once was enough. I simply needed to show you what you had to do, in the most non-threatening way possible.
Three, your father wanted to inherit Ritual Space, but it can only be passed along through the female line. Normally, larger families make this easy, but your father was an only child and you were his only child. In a few decades, you may want to look into fertility spells.

Four, you will live an average of two hundred years. There isn't any getting around it, we live for a very long time and usually leave when we choose. I have always known I was destined for a violent death, so I hope that I have managed to wait until you were over eighteen.

Five, the book is designed to fill you in on all the detailed questions that you may have. Each is grouped by subject. Ask the book, and it should flip to the correct page.

In closing, I wish you had not been dumped into this situation, but feel free to ask the house or the rabbits for anything you need. Mr. Grant will handle the details of my funeral, so put your trust in him. His family has been handling our accounts for centuries.

I love you. I wish you well, and I know you will be fine.

All my love,
Neadra

The rest of the book had an index, tabbed pages and leaves pressed into each one.

She sat and read through the night, the lights of the kitchen came on as daylight faded to nothing. Adrea paused occasionally to have a drink of water, but she didn't feel tired, so she kept reading.

The book was full of family lore as well as a description of how to do a cleanup and renovation of the ritual spaces. The tale of how the spaces had been brought together for the purpose of giving mages somewhere safe to blow up while they were learning. From that point, it turned into a sheltered area for shifters to have events and the mythical beings enjoyed being themselves for days at a time.

How to take bookings was also included in the book. The list of repeat clients could be found in the office along with the other numbers used for the business side of things.

Adrea closed the book and let out a heavy sigh while she ran her hands through her hair. Her mind was spinning with a thousand bits of information, and she needed to sort them out.

She looked down at her clothing and sighed. She should have packed better.

Adrea shoved herself up to her feet, took the book with her and headed up to the third floor where the bedrooms were located. If she was lucky, the house had saved all of Neadra's clothing. Her aunty had been a clotheshorse, and she and Adrea were the same size.

The third door that she opened was Neadra's. The tears started the moment that she set foot over the threshold. Everywhere she looked, she saw her aunty, her mentor and probably her best friend. Just like that, she was gone.

Adrea sat at the edge of the bed and let the sobs come.

Hyl looked up at the rain coming down on the house in the most magical place he had ever been. Adrea Morrigan was finally letting the loss hit her. The rain was the side effect.

He could feel the strength in the containment

of the walls surrounding the space. With the spell holder in control, nothing would be able to breech the defenses.

The strength of the protections just left him with one question as he stood in the shadows of the porch. *How had a killer gotten to Neadra Yoder?*

Adrea woke when the sun tickled her face. Her soul felt lighter for the grieving. There would be more tears, but they wouldn't have the same power as the first wave.

She gathered some exercise gear and looked until she found her room. It was neat, tidy and empty aside from a bed. She located her ensuite bathroom with towels waiting for her, and she took a quick shower to clear her eyes.

Her hair towelled dry in a few seconds, and the moment that her skin wasn't damp, she pulled on spandex shorts and a sports bra. The shoes and socks didn't fit quite right, but then, they weren't hers.

With a deep sigh and a settling sense of grief, she went down two flights of stairs and out the front door.

"You are up early."

She shrieked and jumped to the other side of the porch.

"What the hell, Hyl?" She panted and pressed her hand to her chest. Well, she tried to. She wasn't actually scared at all. Her senses knew that he was there the entire time. She had acted like she would have if she was still completely normal. Normal had been blown up yesterday.

He stepped out of the shadows as if he lived in them, and he inclined his head. "Pardon me. I didn't mean to startle you."

"It is fine. I knew you were there, but I didn't *know* you were there. Did you stay there all night?"

"A sentry spell allows me to remain awake for days at a time."

"Right. Well, I am on my way out for a run. I will be back in an hour or so. Time is funny here."

"I will come with you." He stepped forward.

"I thought you were here to guard the crime scene. I am not going near it."

He paused. "Take your phone and call if you need help."

She shook her head. "No. It throws me off. Just keep an eye out for the rabbits. If they come to get you, you will know I am in trouble. In the meantime, get some rest. From what I hear, those spells aren't good for you."

Adrea turned and started at a gentle run that took her past the house and grounds and into the ritual spaces themselves.

The air changed and cooled as she ran past the standing stones. She cut down a path and headed past the pyramids, the dry and hot air warming as she cut through the desert. From there, she passed the great forest, the haunted forest, the dark forest and the great silent lake.

Scorched ground puffed under her feet through the sterile lands, fading abruptly as she leaped in-

Ritual Space

to the bamboo gardens.

Adrea kept far away from the meditation house. She had the other half of Ritual Space to check, but that could wait a day. She jogged lightly back to her house, and to her disgust, she hadn't even broken a sweat.

Being functionally, temporarily immortal was a pain. She couldn't sweat, couldn't feel fear and her heart rate never went up. No wonder her family lived so long, they couldn't get wound up.

As she glanced at Detective Luning, she wondered if sex would ever be the same again. She knew it wouldn't. How could sex be enjoyable if no one made her heart beat fast?

He blinked and stepped forward. "You have been gone for three hours."

Adrea winced. "Damn. Well, I was doing a tour of my property."

"Mr. Grant and the coroner phoned. They wish you to return their calls."

"Right. I will get right on that." She walked inside and headed to the kitchen. She guzzled three glasses of water and then checked the fridge. She reached in and grabbed an apple, sticking it in her jaws as she headed back to Neadra's room to get some clean clothing. She consumed the apple while she picked out an outfit.

Neadra had a flare for dramatic clothing, so Adrea had a wide range of clothing to choose from. She ended up in a long skirt, button and lace boots and a shirt with a wide cowl neck that showed off most of her shoulders.

She located her phone and winced at the low

battery.

"House, is there a phone-charging cord available?"

There was no answer, so she headed to the office to go through some of the tech boxes that Neadra kept around for curiosities sake. To her amusement, the charging cable she needed was already plugged in next to the computer and waiting for her phone. She plugged it in and looked at the flashing message light on the answering machine.

There were only six messages, so she picked up a pen and piece of paper before playing the messages.

The first was someone who wished to book the space for a family event in a few months. The second was an arcane club who wanted to come and try out a new spell. The third was a hang-up. The fourth was a condolence call as were the last two.

It was so weird to have the calls go from addressing Neadra, to addressing Adrea.

The booking book had columns for each of the environments, so Adrea checked and was able to confirm an available booking for the daughter of the Gangers for their wedding. There would be six hundred guests, so the great field adjoining the bright forest would be in use. She had plenty of room in the booking book, but when she cross-referenced Ganger in the repeat-customer book, it said she needed to book the entire property. Okay, she would.

The spell practice was an easy lock. They wanted the standing stones, so she could definitely fit them in.

With a deliberate manner, she reached out for the phone and called Lenora Ganger back.

"Hello?"

"Hello, Mrs. Ganger? My name is Adrea. I am the new proprietor of Ritual Space."

There was a pause. "My condolences on the loss of Neadra. We have heard and our community mourns."

"Thank you. Well, I don't wish to talk business if you are unready to do so, but if you wish, I have the next full moon from tonight available for that wedding you wish to host. The entire property will be at your disposal, and by then, I should be able to open the gateways you need."

"Thank you. We will be attending the funeral."

"It should be announced shortly. They know what killed her; they just don't know who."

"That is always the one folks have problems with."

"So I am beginning to understand, and we are the ones left behind."

"You have a community who will be there for you, just let us be."

"I look forward to meeting you in person. Consider February the twenty-second yours."

"Thank you. Have a serene day."

"Be tranquil and serene."

Adrea hung up the phone and felt a little bit better.

The next call was all business. She explained that it would be two weeks before she could take in a client, and the caller hung up on her.

"Well, that was easy."

She checked on her phone, and the charge was complete. It showed the two missing calls. "Huh, they must have called Hyl."

She contacted the coroner, and she was told that the body of her aunt was ready to be released. They had obtained all the information they could from her.

The call to Mr. Grant confirmed that he was having the body picked up and handled according to Neadra's wishes. The funeral would be announced later in the day.

He asked Adrea if she would get the clothing for Neadra to be buried in, and Adrea agreed. He would send a courier in a few hours, and she would have the clothing ready for him.

The calls were relatively easy on her. She trotted upstairs and picked out the outfit that Neadra had pointed out a dozen times as the one she wanted to be buried in. Neadra had been born in Victorian times and wanted to wear her dress complete with bustle and hook and eye boots. She would go out in her beautiful bottle-blue outfit, and the silk would make her glow.

Adrea smiled as she packed the clothing in a small suitcase with care to keep the lines straight. Neadra was fussy about her appearance; it wouldn't do to have wrinkles.

She latched the case closed and carried it downstairs. After this, there was the funeral. She couldn't do anything else for Neadra but find her killer.

With her mind turning cold, she set the case

down in her living room and headed outside. It was time to face the murder scene.

Chapter Six

The detective was right behind her as she stood on the wide deck surrounding the meditation house.

"This was supposed to be a peaceful place. It was supposed to give people a sense of serenity. That someone invaded this space to take her life is nearly sacrilege." She spoke to him but didn't look at him.

The crime-scene tape was gone, if it had ever been there. From the moment she had identified the site, she hadn't looked at it. The blonde wood door and bamboo panels gave the feeling of lightness to the space.

"You do not have to do this. The investigators are finished with the space, but crime-scene clean-up can be called."

Adrea shook her head and kept her focus on the door that could not lock. "No they can't. When I have confirmed that there is no further value to this property, it will be absorbed and a new meditation site will be here. It will be a good spot, a clear spot to commune with one's soul again."

His voice seemed surprised. "You will destroy

it?"

"I will do nothing. I will simply tell the property that it no longer serves its intended purpose. It will take care of the rest."

She inhaled and exhaled slowly. With a stiff posture, she took a step into the brightly lit building where her aunt had breathed her last.

Detective Luning followed her.

The marks left by blood struck her as if she was feeling those same strikes to her torso again. She fell to her knees but kept conscious.

In her mind, she could see a dark figure. It was the soul she was seeing and not the body. That was the point of the meditation house; it showed you the state of your soul.

"Are you all right?"

"Yes. I am just dealing with the attack. I can't believe it was only yesterday."

"Well, without your call, she wouldn't have been found, and we wouldn't have been able to begin the investigation."

She caught her breath and tasted the blood in the air. "Glad to help."

The marks that Adrea could still feel had all been delivered with Neadra standing on her feet.

"What are you thinking? Say it out loud."

She glanced at the detective and blinked at what she saw. A kernel of white energy was surrounded by grey and a thin line of black. She had never seen an aura like that before.

Adrea rose and walked to a few feet away from where Neadra had been stabbed. "She was kneeling in her daily meditation. I run, she meditated."

Adrea knelt and mimicked her aunt's pose. It was like she could feel her aunt with them.

"The door opens."

Adrea turned her head toward the door, but she kept her eyes closed, seeing the memory that wasn't hers as it happened.

"It is someone she knows, but she has never seen him like this. His aura is dark. Midnight black shot with poison green. She gets on her feet to greet him, and he rushes in, blade out."

She was on her feet now and swaying. "The first strike of the three was enough to kill her, but she hangs on. She laughs at him. It won't get him what he wants. Nothing can. The next two strikes are in anger, and she falls."

She dragged another breath in and waited for the fading of the pain that would tell her that her aunt was dead.

She looked to Detective Luning. "Will they tell me when this place can be removed?"

"I will make sure of it."

"Good. She is still here. Traces of her. Her death is not the part of her I wish to remember. I want to remember her life."

He nodded and seemed to come to a decision. He put his arm around her shoulders and escorted her out of the building.

She leaned into him and relaxed for a moment before following his lead. Outside, the smell of blood lingered in her nostrils for a moment, and then, she clenched her fists.

"It was a male. Six foot one. He is a mage or has recently been doing spell work. He had rage

Ritual Space

against her. Wanted something from her, and she laughed and said he would never get it. That amusement that she felt was real. She was exceptionally ladylike, but that was her *fuck you*."

He chuckled. "I will call the guild the moment you are settled. When did you last eat?"

She frowned. "I had an apple before my run, I think. I don't need much food. The property feeds me."

"You need solid food. Come on. I will see what I can find."

He shepherded her into her home and to the table in the kitchen. He held her chair for her and went to the fridge.

"Why are you being nice to me?" She propped her head on her fist and watched him assemble ingredients for an omelette.

"You are a witness and a victim, of sorts. It was also pointed out to me that this property is a vital source of practice for the guild. Your aunt used to allow the guild to take it over for a few days and run spell games. Practicing attack and defense."

Adrea smiled. "She would never let me be here for those days. She was worried about me interfering or falling in love with a young mage defending his team. She had a very romantic view of the world and was constantly on guard against romantic love."

He whisked the eggs together, and he pulled out a frying pan. "Iron?"

"Specially made cast iron. It is bog iron that has been melted once and made into a pan. It isn't suitable for anything other than cookware, but it works just fine. Brittle though. I broke one once when I was seven or eight. I got a lecture, and Neadra took me to the forge to watch it being melted and remade."

"So, what is the deal with metal?"

"It is multiple things in the same body. Neadra couldn't use them. Everything here has a single source. Plastic is the only exception."

"Why is that?"

"Because it isn't something when it is broken down to its components. The chemicals are liquid and gas but nothing usable or natural on their own. It can be burned into a gaseous—if toxic—form with little effort."

"Extremely odd."

She chuckled as he stood by the oven. "You work with the Mage Guild. Odd is in your daily activities. When will you be ready to leave here and return to your normal duties?"

"Tired of me already?" He glanced at her with a smile.

"It isn't that. This is hardly a dangerous situation."

"Are you sure about that? A person known to your aunt walked up to her and stabbed her in the chest and had enough magical skill to fake it as a suicide here in the house."

He poured the eggs into the pan. "If they didn't get what they wanted from her, they might try and get it from you."

She shivered and hugged herself while he loaded the veg and cheese into the pan.

"I had been trying not to think of that."

"There will be an officer or detective of the Mage Guild or the XIA here around the clock until this murder is solved."

"The XIA?"

"Yes, they have a history here as well. I believe some of their members enjoy this facility as well."

"Well, they are on the approved-client list. I just have never had any exposure to them. Do they really have teams that use at least three branches of the extranormal population?"

"They do. I have worked with a few of the local teams as a human counterpoint. They work very well in their unit."

She nodded. "Okay. I can deal with that. Mr. Grant said that the body was released today. He is going to be sending someone by to get clothing for her. I picked out one of her favourite outfits."

He got a plate and expertly folded the omelette out onto the wooden surface. He set it in front of her with a flourish, and she smiled. "Thank you."

He explored a little and found the forks. It was a lesser flourish, but still impressive. She took the fork and repeated her thanks.

The food was pretty good. It needed some seasoning, perhaps some fresh herbs, but other than that, it was just what her body needed. She could almost hear her cells shrieking with relief. Adrea might be able to survive on the energy of the property, but her body didn't like it.

Detective Luning got a call while she was eating, and when she set her fork down, he asked her, "Is there a way for Mr. Grant's assistant to get into the gate?"

"Oh, of course." She released the front gate. "It's open."

Adrea got to her feet and quickly washed her plate and the utensils that the detective had used. When the knock sounded at the front door, she set everything on the draining board and followed Luning to the front door.

He opened the door and asked the young gargoyle woman for identification. She turned her arm over and showed the glyph that marked her as one of the Granite clan. Adrea smiled and got the suitcase.

"Thank you for coming. Here are the clothes that I think she would have chosen."

"Thank you, Ms. Morrigan. Do you have a preference for her hairstyle?"

Adrea smiled. "She was always partial to a Gibson Girl."

The woman smiled and pressed her palm to Adrea's shoulder. "I am sure that Harkox Funeral Home can manage it. My grief joins yours. Neadra was a wonderful woman."

"I didn't get your name."

"Gera. Gera Grant. I work for my father. This is my direct line. Call me if you need anything. My father has stated that I am to be at your beck and call."

Adrea took the proffered card. "Thank you, but I don't want to abuse anyone's good nature."

Gera grinned. "I get paid for it. Don't worry. Ritual Space is one of our family's oldest, if not *the* oldest client. It is a profitable account and requires very little effort. We deserve to work a little."

Adrea thought for a second. "Well, if you don't mind, I will text you a grocery and clothing list. You should have it by the time you are back in town."

"No problem. Did you want us to pack up your apartment and bring everything here?"

Adrea was stunned. "You can do that?"

"Of course. We are acting on behalf of your corporation. We can do all kinds of stuff."

"Definitely. Definitely bring all my stuff."

Gera laughed. "Text me so I have a specific order to attach the bill to, and I will do your bidding. We can have your wardrobe here by the end of the day. Faster, if you can open a gateway."

"I haven't done that yet."

"You have to start sometime." Gera shrugged. "It was lovely meeting you, and I look forward to working with you in the future."

The gargoyle bowed, flaring her wings out, and she left with the suitcase in hand.

Luning closed the door, and he raised his brows. "You look excited."

"I will have my own underwear for tomorrow morning. You have no idea how happy I am right now."

With a grin, she dashed upstairs, heading for her phone with the business card clutched in her fingers.

It was time to start working on making this place her home and not just her prison.

Chapter Seven

"Mr. Grant explained the situation to the captain, so he will be sending someone to question you again."

Adrea looked up from her frantic texting, and she nodded while her thumbs continued to work.

"Okay. Whatever I can do to help. As long as Mr. Grant knows I am being questioned."

"Confirm it with him if you like. He has agreed to it as you have a rock-solid alibi, being in public and rushed to hospital, as you were."

She grimaced and looked down at her screen, adding the question to her note to Gera.

"Okay. There. She has a list of essentials. Now that you have woken my stomach, it is making demands."

Her phone chimed.

Yes, Father authorized them to talk to you. They are looking for suspects, so give them anyone who has acted out of character.

Adrea smiled at Luning. "Yeah, I am good to talk to them. For now, I need to check the book. I have to figure out how to open a gateway."

She returned to her aunt's room and picked up

the book, carrying it to her own bedroom. She sat on the bed and read the directions on how to allow those who were distant to come through to the property.

It was simple. She merely had to let herself relax and feel the knocking and then answer the door. Invited persons would always text or call first, and from there, she would know to stand in the arrivals' yard to open the gate.

It seemed easy, and Adrea definitely hoped it was.

She closed the book and left it on her bed, heading downstairs. She was on the second flight when she felt a punch to the abdomen. Something was in the property and trying to get out.

She gripped the railing and groaned as the agony tore through her again.

Luning was at her side in seconds, and he lifted her up, carrying her down the stairs to the living room, setting her on one of the couches while she fought what was going on.

She gripped Luning's hand as the pain tried again. This time, she tensed and forced it down, slamming it back.

She sat up and closed her eyes, looking for the source of the pain. Flashes of the dark forest appeared in her mind, a small altar and a few herbs were next to a coiling mist of darkness.

The moment she was under control, she murmured. "I need to check something."

"I am coming with you."

She shrugged. "As you like."

She set her phone to vibrate and left the house,

heading for the main gates. Her bike was there. She was going to need it to catch that wisp of smoke before it disappeared.

She got on, started it up and looked at Luning with challenge in her eyes. "If you want to come along, get on."

He scowled and got on behind her.

She smiled as she clued in to the fact that he hadn't been on a bike before. "Arms around my waist, feet up on the pegs. Lean when I lean."

His long arms wrapped around her waist, and she paused at the feel of him against her back. That was a lot of muscle.

Adrea got herself back to the mission, and they were away, ripping down the trails and through the property to the dark woods.

Luning did pretty good. He only threw her off balance a few times. When she rumbled the bike to a halt and put the stand down, he eagerly hopped off.

She chuckled and followed him.

"What are we doing?"

"I am looking for the altar and the dark spirit that has been trying to claw his way out of me." She sighed. "I mean, out of the property."

"And you decided to come here without back-up?"

"I have you."

"Before I invited myself along."

She winced. "Yes?"

He sighed. "Which way?"

Adrea closed her eyes and looked into the darkness. "There."

She walked into the dark woods with confidence, sliding her body through narrow gaps in trees. How he managed to follow her, she didn't know, but Luning was behind her every step of the way.

"How can you see where you are going?"

"This is me. Apparently, this is my lower abdomen."

She heard him chuckle and had to admit it sounded funny.

After pressing through the thick woods, they stumbled into the clearing. There it was where it shouldn't have been. The altar and the herbs were together, just like in her vision.

The column of mist wasn't there anymore, but she wanted to remove all parts of the altar.

"Something was summoned in the hours that there was no curator. It managed to crack a window, and it is still trying to fight its way into this world."

"What will happen if you destroy the altar?"

"Nothing. It was a focus to make the crack between worlds. The problem is how to do it? I can't use magic, so that is out; I guess I can ask the forest to do it."

"I could shatter it with magic."

Adrea looked at him in the shadows and smiled. "You are a detective, not a demolition man. This is my world now. I need to get used to asking it for what I need."

"Very well. I am here if you need me."

Adrea flexed her hands and tried to remember what Neadra had written. She knelt next to the altar made of marble bricks. She made her hands into claws and thrust them into the ground, asking for what she wanted.

There was silence for a moment, and then, the dark forest rustled. Coils of stiff tendrils crept from the soil and locked into the foreign object. They grew around it, and a crack made Adrea move back. The next moment, the altar disappeared in a puff of rock dust and flying shards.

Adrea braced for the impact of the shards, but a barrier manifested at the moment of explosion.

Luning was at her side, his hand extended, and it was obviously his magic holding back the continued breakage of the rocks as the vines tore it apart and pulled the pieces deep into the ground.

Her companion sighed and slowly lowered the shield. "So, you didn't really have a plan."

She looked at the pale shards being consumed by the woods around them. "Not really."

"Well, do you need to blow up the herbs as well?"

She frowned. "No. I am going to look into what they were summoning. There isn't anything out here and a trip to the dark forest isn't something folks normally engage in. There are other environments that are more suitable to this kind of thing, but this one provides the best concealment."

"You just answered your question."

Adrea nodded and got to her feet, brushing her hands on her thighs. She sent a mental thank you to the trees around her, and the following rustle told her that they had answered. "Weird."

"What?"

"I am still getting used to the idea that I have been fused to the world around me on a permanent basis."

"I imagine it takes some getting used to."

"You have no idea." She walked over to the plant segments and looked at the leaves. "This isn't right."

"What? What does it summon?"

"Nothing. This is a collection of herbs to use in a stew. They are tasty, but no mage could do more with this than increase or open breathing passages."

She asked the forest to consume it, and when she heard the sharp sound of glass breaking, she looked closer. A sharp spike of glass had been contained in the bouquet.

"Oh, my. Okay, that was unexpected."

Luning leaned over her shoulder. "What was it?"

"A spike of glass. It looks like one of the ceremonial daggers that my aunt has in a display case. I will look for it when we go back to the house. If that was meant for me, this is much more serious."

She turned and headed back to the motorcycle. He was right behind her.

Her hands were shaking as she gripped the handles of the bike. He didn't say anything, merely wrapped his arms around her, and soon, they were off.

She parked outside the house and headed into the living room, looking into the flat, framed display of ornamental daggers.

Luning was amazed. "How did I not see that before?"

"I didn't want them on display. They are all cursed and very deadly."

"Cursed?"

"Oh, yeah. Lives and souls have been taken by these. Damn. It is missing."

"What is?"

"The drainer of magic and souls. The Tyima dagger. The smallest nick of that glass can drain a body of everything and leave it a hollow shell."

He looked sick. "That was just lying out there?"

She swallowed. "It was."

"How do you know about it?"

Adrea looked at the missing spot in the display case. "I studied all of these daggers when I was here during the summers. Sending me to Ritual Space was like sending me to camp, but it was free."

"And you chose to read up on cursed daggers?"

"Sure. I went through a morbid phase that thankfully ended when Blueberry arrived. He was going to be sacrificed to help a woman get pregnant, but she couldn't kill him and that is what helped her spell. She sent Neadra flowers at the beginning of the next summer."

Luning blinked. "Why does he have a blue streak?"

"I honestly thought that would have rubbed off by now, but I was making blueberry pie and crushing blueberries for a sauce to put over the pie and ice cream when it was done and he came hopping in. I splashed the hot blueberry sauce on his little head."

She wrinkled her nose. "Neadra wiped his head and washed him off, but the blue turned bright, and it stayed. She said it was fate marking him. I thought I was just clumsy."

Adrea fought a smile when she realized how quickly Luning could distract her. It was a skill of his, and she was beginning to appreciate it.

She thought about Blueberry and how he should have been long gone by now. It was less than thirty seconds until he was hopping up next to her. She cuddled him and relaxed at the feel of the small, warm body.

Luning got a call, and he spoke softly. When he hung up, he said, "The detective is at the gates."

She nodded and opened the gate. "He can come in."

He smiled brightly. "Excellent. Did you want to meet him here?"

"I will be out on the porch."

"Good. Is Blueberry coming with us?"

"He is." She held him, and he settled against her with a dignity peculiar to blue-splashed bunnies.

She walked out to the porch and took a seat on the swing. She was gently rocking back and forth when the detective walked up the steps.

She smiled. "Good afternoon."

Luning made the introductions. "Detective Rells, this is the curator of Ritual Space, Adrea Morrigan."

Detective Rells smiled; his blond hair gleamed with health and his dark-brown eyes sparkled. "I am pleased to meet you, Ms. Morrigan. May I ask you some questions?"

"Sure. My lawyer has okayed it, so ask your questions." She stroked Blueberry's head and smiled vacantly.

Luning was staring at her in astonishment, and a smirk began to form on his lips when the questioning started.

"Do you know who killed Neadra Yoder?"

"No."

"What do you know about her death?" He leaned forward, his notepad out and his pen at the ready.

Adrea sighed. "She was killed by someone she knew. He stabbed her. After that, she told him that he could not get what he wanted, and then, she laughed at him. He stabbed her two more times."

"How do you know this?"

Adrea sighed and kept stroking Blueberry. "Because I went to where she was killed and the building showed me. The meditation house is not arranged for holding a soul, but it didn't like the violence or the blood."

"The building showed you?"

"Yes. You are a mage; you can wiggle your fingers and summon dinner. Is it so weird that a building connected to the most serene places on earth would not like getting a murder on that serenity?"

Luning laughed before he stifled his amusement.

Rells made a few more notes before asking her the questions she had been waiting for.

chapter eight

"Do you know of anyone who wished your aunt ill?"

Adrea nodded. "Well, there is the curator of Enchanted Valley; she didn't like Neadra. That is probably because she is trying to start up a new version of this kind of a space and she isn't very good at it."

Rells nodded. "Anyone else?"

"My father. He wanted to inherit this space, but that was never going to happen."

Rells perked up. "He is the eldest in the family?"

"Oh, yes. But he isn't suitable to take this place over."

"Why not?" Rells was writing frantically.

"He's male. Ritual Space can only be run by a woman. It is the way it has always been. The land fits into our lives neatly. There is no chance for that to happen with a male."

Luning asked, "Has it ever been tried?"

"Yes. Once. Neadra told me that he had gone mad within a week. The family had to kill him and give the property to his sister. It was not our finest hour."

"When was this?"

She squinted, "I believe it was in the sixteenth century."

"Oh. Okay. So, your father thinks that Ritual Space is his right?"

"He used to. I mean, he was pretty mad at me in the hospital."

"Hospital?"

"Oh. I was working in a teashop when Neadra was stabbed. I felt every strike, and I passed out. I woke up in the hospital with my hair and eye colour altered and knowledge that I was needed at Ritual Space."

"What did your father say?"

"He asked how long that I knew I was Neadra's inheritor. He was furious that I was wearing the sign of inheriting the property. My mother just stared at me without saying anything."

Rells gave her a commiserating look. "That must have been difficult."

"Not nearly as bad as Christmas. That was rather ugly." She realized something. "I must have been out of it for a while. My parents live in Arberg."

Rells looked surprised. "I thought you lived in Danforth."

"I do; they don't. It was why it was so convenient for them to bring me here for the summers. It was half an hour away."

She cocked her head. "Is there a record of how they got to Danforth so quickly?"

Rells nodded. "After you were taken to hospital,

there was an emergency transport for them."

"Okay. That explains it. I am just amazed that they came. Last year, I had appendicitis, and they didn't show up. Neadra did, but my parents didn't."

Rells inclined his head. "Right. Do you know anyone else who might have had ill feelings toward your aunt?"

"I have a list of folks who are barred from the property, but it couldn't have been any of them."

"Why not?"

Adrea looked at him and realized he wasn't keeping up. "She wouldn't have let them through the gates. Her killer was either someone that she let in or someone who could force his way in without her feeling it."

Luning chipped in, "Someone either very familiar or very powerful."

Rells scribbled it down on his notepad.

Adrea stroked Blueberry and waited for the next question.

"So, do you hate your parents? Did you manipulate Neadra Yoder into naming you her heir?" He had gone from affable to intense.

She blinked, and her mouth opened in surprise. "Um, no, I don't hate my parents. I don't like them, and they don't like me but that isn't unusual. As for Neadra, she chose me. My attorney has the details, but she chose me as the most suitable family member to take over this property and all it entails. I give you authorization to quiz Mr. Grant for any information on the matter that he is willing to give up."

"You accepted this property, knowing it would

create a rift between you and your parents?"

She stared at him intently. "I felt my aunt murdered, I woke up in hospital with the marks of this place on me. I wasn't given a choice to accept or hand it off to someone else. It doesn't work that way."

Blueberry was vibrating with irritation. It was coming off him in waves. Adrea heard a low growl, and she looked down at the bunny. His ears were back and his teeth were exposed.

"Detective, you have worn out your welcome."

He looked to Luning, but the other detective shrugged. "She is speaking to you as a courtesy, and you have just stepped over the line."

Adrea got to her feet. "I am only going to talk with Detective Luning or members of the XIA in the future. The Mage Guild at large is sorely disappointing."

"Ms. Morrigan, that is not your call."

She smiled tightly. "As curator of Ritual Space, it is. I am sure they will be more than capable of investigating this, and I would dearly love someone who had already met my aunt to come in and talk about her with me. It seems the mages just liked to use the property for their own ends."

She stepped toward him, forcing him to back toward the stairs of the porch. "Goodbye."

Rells stepped back and stumbled as the herd of bunnies moved to trip him.

"The captain will call you."

She smirked. "I am sure he will. I don't give a rat's ass. This place is split between jurisdictions. I am not a mage, but I am not quite a human. Yeah, the XIA is what I want investigating this."

The bunnies screwed with him the entire way back to the gate. She locked the property the moment he left. The rabbits flooded back, and she resumed her comfortable seat on the porch swing.

Luning was rubbing his face, and his phone was in his hand. "Yes, sir. No, sir. Well, it was when Rells told her that she schemed to get control of the property, sir. Give the team my number, and we will be waiting." He hung up.

"Is this going to get you in trouble?"

He chuckled. "No. Rells is another matter. He is about to get a lecture on the etiquette of dealing with the bereaved when those members inherit ancient, powerful magic bestowed by the deceased years before they met their end."

"I wonder if he will understand."

"Whether he does or not, you are getting your wish. The XIA is getting the murder, and they are far more interested in finding an answer than the mages are."

She stroked Blueberry's chin. "It will give you a chance to take a break and go do whatever it is that you do when you are not skulking in shadows."

He chuckled. "I live in the shadows."

Adrea looked at him with her limited knowledge and came to a conclusion. "You are not completely human."

"Nope. I will give you five bucks and go for burgers if you guess right."

She frowned and then grinned. In her thoughts, she forwarded her request to the bunnies. They swarmed his feet, sniffing and examining.

Luning smirked. "That is cheating."

Innocently, she looked at him, making her eyes as wide as possible. "What is? The bunnies just want to say hey."

The rabbits sent back images of trees, images of rock and a babbling brook.

Every child was taught the basic families of extranaturals or extranormals. She could only guess at, "Mountain nymph?"

His eyes widened. "In all my years, no one has ever guessed that."

She sighed. "Fine, but am I right?"

He winked. "I will let you know after I take my break."

The answer was going to have to wait.

It was dusk before the XIA arrived, which made sense as they had nocturnal team members. Luning had gotten a call and wandered off half an hour ago. Adrea had been enjoying her moment of silence.

He returned to the porch and smiled. "They are here."

She blinked. "I know. Someone is knocking."

"Knocking? I don't hear anything."

She tapped the side of her head. "In here. I recognize the request, and they are on their way in."

"Recognize it?"

She gave him a look. "It is all new to me, but the property recognizes them, so they are coming in."

Blueberry scrambled off her lap and made for

the shrubs with the rest of his people.

"I am guessing that a predator is on the way." She got to her feet and brushed her hands over her skirt.

Luning headed down the steps when the three men appeared on the path.

Adrea was about to join him when her phone buzzed. The caller ID told her it was Gera.

"Hello?"

"Hello, Adrea. I am ready to send things through if you want to go to the reception area and open the gateway."

"Oh. Sure. I will head right out." She hung up and grinned, trying not to clap excitedly.

She was down the stairs and sprinting past the gathering of men a moment later. "Sorry, Luning. My stuff is here."

The skirt was a little tight as she ran, but her quick stepping got her to the arrival area in three minutes.

The pressing on her mind was definitely a request for access. She skidded to a halt and focused on a point a few dozen metres away. With a deep breath, she authorized the entry and watched the magic gateway appear.

The XIA officers and Luning were behind her as the moving team began to haul her clothing and possessions through the gate. Three additional gargoyles were assisting and moving her items in large quantities.

Gera smiled and thanked them when the pile was in Ritual Space. She remained in the space while the others returned through the gateway.

Adrea denied access to the gate, and it closed. "Huh. So that is how that works."

Gera grinned. "I will bring this into your house."

Luning cleared his throat. "We can help."

The men looked at him in surprise and then shrugged. The golden man with dark hair and pointed ears chuckled. "Sure. We can ask questions on the way."

The boxes were marked and very heavy, but Gera and the others managed to haul them all into the house in about twenty minutes.

Gera inclined her head. "I will be on my way. Will you let me out of your airspace?"

"Oh. Sure. Of course." Adrea frowned. "Remain low over the wall. I will open a window for you."

"Excellent. Well, gentlemen, it has been delightful sweating with you." Gera winked, extended her wings and took to the sky.

Adrea watched her and focused on opening a window about twenty feet square, right in front of Gera.

When Gera was gone and the energy was back where it should be, Adrea turned to the XIA. "Introductions?"

Luning sighed. "This is Agent Kel, Agent Hix and Agent Dark."

The vampire bowed. "My name was originally Dirk, but my maker asked me to change it. Dark is my current designation."

Hix smiled. "I have offered my services to the XIA because I am a people person."

Kel snorted. "And he is a gryphon. I am but a

simple elf."

Adrea inclined her head. "I am a shut-in dependent on the good graces of those such as yourselves to find my aunt's killer. Have you read the file?"

Hix nodded. "We have, and we knew Neadra. She spoke fondly of you at every opportunity."

Adrea relaxed. "Well, in that case. Thank you for coming. Would you like to see the crime scene?"

The men looked at each other in the glow of the porch light, and they nodded as one.

It was time to return to the meditation house, and this time, do it right.

Chapter Nine

It was almost fun to watch the XIA agents at work. The shifter sniffed, the undead examined the blood and the fey closed his eyes to sense the energy around him.

Adrea kept herself outside the door to reduce the chance of them seeing her aura. She was a little embarrassed by it.

Luning was next to her, watching the agents move around the space to get the sense of it.

She had to ask, "So you have worked with them before?"

"Yes. They are the team I am most often sent out with."

She nodded. "So you trust them?"

"I do."

"Then, go and take a break. I will be fine. Since our foray into the woods, I feel all right."

Luning made a face and then nodded. He went in and spoke to the agents. When they seemed to agree with him, he left, whispered, "Behave," and disappeared into the shadows again.

Adrea could feel him in the area, but she couldn't see him. It was odd. It was as if he melted into the shadows around them, and at this time of night, there were plenty.

Kel turned toward her. "Can you come in and describe the events?"

She winced. "I can relive them. This is the last time I will do it. I have felt the death enough."

Hix nodded. "We understand."

Dark gestured. "Come in; we don't bite. We have all eaten this evening."

She snorted. "That is not what I am worried about."

She stepped forward and looked at them through the filter of the meditation house. Hix burned gold with flickering flames of dark impulses.

Kel was a cool green-gold with a light fuzzing of grey around him in a halo and Dark was not. A brilliant scarlet with bright flares of white streaking across it. She could not have imagined that result. Aside from the blood lust, he was a really good guy. No wonder Hyl trusted them.

She settled where she had knelt earlier and opened her mind to the space around her.

Her aunt's soul walked her through the murder again. She could see the agents behind the shadow as she spoke to it and got to her feet. When the stab came, she swayed and taunted her attacker. As the final thrust struck her abdomen, she dropped heavily to her knees.

Kel was watching the spectre of her aunt die, but Hix took action. He lifted her and carried her out of the meditation house.

She dragged in a deep breath. "Thanks for that."

"Not a problem. You are having an exhausting week."

She chuckled weakly. "This is day two. I can only imagine what the weekend will bring."

"Don't speculate. It could be complicated."

Adrea nodded and leaned her head against his shoulder before she realized what she was doing. She jerked upright with a jolt. "Sorry."

"For what? You are exhausted. We told Hyl we would take care of you. So, we will. Relax and rest if you can."

She shuddered and relaxed in his arms. Sleep overcame her. It had been one murder too many.

Voices were murmuring around her, and she sat upright. She was on the couch in the living room, and the agents and Luning were in the room with her, holding a low discussion of what they had seen.

Light skimmed through the drawn drapes. Dark was sitting in a corner, cuddling with Blueberry. In fact, all of her fluffy companions were in the room. Hix had a large grey rabbit in his lap, and Kel was stroking two tiny whites.

Luning was cradling a large brown rabbit as he leaned against the fireplace. He smiled at her, "Good morning."

Kel got to his feet and went into the kitchen with two bunnies in one hand. When he returned, he had a glass of water and two content companions still with him.

She smiled. "Thanks. Good morning. I hadn't realized how tired I was."

Hix nodded. "You have engaged in a transformation. It is hard on the body. Believe me."

She laughed. "I believe you." Adrea gulped the water down in seconds.

Kel asked her, "Would you like to know what we saw?"

She set the glass down on a table that hadn't been there a moment earlier. She was surprised that there wasn't a coaster, and then, there it was. She laughed. "Yes, please. Tell me what you saw."

Dark lifted his head and spoke in a drowsy voice. "There is evil stalking this place. It hungers for power, and it wants freedom. I know both of those sensations very well."

Kel nodded. "I sensed power, old and twisted. It was driving the evil."

Hix quirked his lips and cocked his head. "And I saw two creatures fused with power. One had surrendered to it, and the other was merely wrapped in it. Neadra was vulnerable because the property had not invested itself in her."

Adrea stared at him. "What?"

"I know melded beings. It is sort of my thing. The Neadra that I saw in that projection was not fully melded to the power that she controlled. It was a tool, and she was the curator of this property, but she was not completely part of it."

"That isn't possible. She was the curator here for over a century."

Hix shrugged. "I know what I see, and you have the same level of amalgamation that she did. The property is listening to you, but it has not joined with you."

She rubbed her forehead. "Right. I am going to have to look into that."

Hyl nodded. "I can call the guild and see if there is anyone who can offer advice on this."

Kel chipped in, "Call the Gangers. They have access to nearly every magical document on the east side of the continent. Now that Benny is an agent for the XIA, they are eager to share their knowledge."

Hyl scowled. "I have not met her team yet."

Hix grinned. "I will make the call. I have been to the Ganger home for a few events. Emile is a charming... man."

The gryphon got to his feet and walked into the kitchen, pulling out his phone as he went.

The room fell silent with only the light snuffling of the bunnies.

Hix returned and sat down. "They are happy to help. They will find all the information on the curators of Ritual Space and bring it to you, as you are currently confined."

"Lenora Ganger?" Adrea blinked.

"Yes. Have you met her?"

"No, but I have spoken to her. She is arranging her daughter's wedding." She got to her feet and walked up to her office, retrieving the booking book.

"Here. In two weeks, Lenora Ganger booked the entire property for her daughter's wedding. Funny, I hadn't realized it. It had already been written and then erased." She sat and tapped the page.

Hix chuckled. "They had to go on a covert mission. It wasn't sure that they would be home in time. If she booked it again, they are definitely going to be back."

Kel grinned. "Excellent. It is going to be quite the party."

Dark chuckled. "We will probably be working."

Hix sighed. "Sorry."

Adrea frowned. "Why can't you get the evening off?"

Kel snickered. "Because Hix isn't affected by the full moon like some of the agents are. We work a lot of full moons."

"Ah. Well, I hope that I don't have to do anything other than open the gates for that night. I am clueless."

Luning smiled. "It will be fine."

She flipped through the book and checked the long-term bookings. "Huh."

Luning cocked his head. "What?"

"I was sure that the Mage Guides would camp out here now and then."

Dark chuckled. "They are afraid that one of their little ones would wander off and get eaten by something."

Adrea snorted. "Not likely. Not unless the bunnies go feral."

Her stomach growled, and Luning nodded. "Right. I will go on a grocery run. Time to get things normalized around here."

She smiled, found her phone and sent him a fast text with her shopping list.

He looked down, raised his brows and shook his head. "I don't know if I can find this many herbs."

She wrinkled her nose. "I can take a look in the gardens. I was just never allowed to fuss with them when I was little. Find what you can, and I will look for the others."

He nodded and left.

The moment she let him out of the property, she looked at the three XIA agents. "Okay, what the hell is Luning?"

Dark grinned, Kel looked surprised and Hix cackled.

Hix asked, "You spotted that, did you?"

"We were in the meditation house. I can see all of your auras, and his was a little odd."

Hix snorted. "It would be. He is a mage, but he is from Sekron."

She rubbed her forehead and tried to remember her geography. "The city of shadows and death?"

Kel looked surprised all over again. "Yes."

Dark laughed. "That is where I met Luning a few years ago. My maker is in the king's court, and I was working security. The king hired Luning to take out a few of those who threatened his reign. They were quickly and quietly dealt with."

That should have surprised her, but she had seen it. "He's an assassin."

Hix piped up, "And law enforcement."

"Okay. I can deal with that. As long as I am not on his agenda, I have no problem with it."

Hix chuckled. "I wouldn't say you aren't on his agenda, but you aren't in any danger."

Kel snorted. "By the way. Nice call getting us in here instead of the mages. They are not very accepting of other forms of magic."

Adrea shrugged. "It was a reflex. I knew that something magical had killed her, so it was where my brain went. I don't have a lot of exposure to the XIA in my daily life."

Dark looked at her with his sleepy gaze. "What do you do?"

"I did work at a tea and herb shop. Now, I hang out here." She got to her feet. "That reminds me, I am going to check and see what the gardens have to offer."

Kel sighed. "I will go with you."

She chuckled. "I am just going out back. There isn't any danger unless the bunnies revolt."

The elf didn't comment but remained on her heels.

She walked into the bright morning sun and inhaled the green scents of the garden.

"This is impressive."

"Neadra was an avid gardener. I am far more interested in the herbs and leaves than fruits and vegetables."

She walked through the garden and to the drying shed, pulling out a small obsidian knife and walking around Kel back toward the herb patch.

She cut some lavender, some chamomile and a bit of lemon balm.

Kel watched her as she continued to harvest far more than she needed.

When she got up and carried the bundles to the drying shed, he caught on.

"You are going to dry them."

"I am. I am also going to source seeds for other

plants that I am used to dealing with. I am also going to make a pot of tea with these fresh herbs, but it will be a little different than the one made from dry."

"Fresher?"

"Less flavourful. It is weird, but I prefer the dried plants for tea."

She tied off the three bundles and hung them from the rack suspended from the ceiling for that purpose. The handful of herbs left was gathered, and she was going to return to the house when a doorbell rang in her head.

"What the hell?" She followed the energy pattern of the sound and approached the meeting grounds with Kel at her back again.

To her astonishment, when she opened the portal that was knocking, a demon walked out.

Chapter Ten

The demon was carrying two armloads of books and a charming woman was holding onto his arm.

"I apologize. Ever since he got free, his demon form has been activated by the touch of strange magic. Once he is used to you, it won't happen. Hello, Adrea. I am Lenora Ganger. This is my husband, Harcourt."

Adrea blinked. "Pleased to meet you."

She stepped forward and offered her hand to Lenora and then to, when he shifted the weight of the books to one arm for a moment, Harcourt. The moment she touched him, he became a debonair human male.

She smiled. "Well, the suit makes more sense now."

He grinned. "Thank you for your calm. I have had a few recent issues with my appearance. It is slowly coming under my control, but I can't guarantee it from one day to the next."

Lenora wiped a tear from her cheek. "You look just like her."

"The magic took care of that. I used to be a

brunette. Would you care to join me inside? I see you have a wide selection of books, and I would love to see what you have brought me."

Harcourt inclined his head. "Lead the way."

She turned, and Kel was right behind her. He held out his arms to Harcourt. "Mr. Ganger. I can help with that."

"Thank you, Kel." Harcourt dumped half the books on him, and as a group, they walked back to the house.

"Let's go in the back. I have a vampire napping in the living room, and I don't want to sear him with sunlight."

Lenora chuckled. "Dark is sturdier than that."

"You know them?"

Harcourt chuckled. "Hix brought his team over to the last family barbeque. He's Lenora's cousin four times removed."

She nodded. "Right. Of course."

Lenora grinned. "You will get used to it. The magical community is surprisingly inbred."

Kel piped up, "Just look at Benny."

Harcourt demoned out for a moment before he calmed. "Sorry. Still getting used to that. Don't insult my daughter, Kel."

"No insult intended, Mr. Ganger. Benny is one of a kind."

Adrea led the way around the back and in through the garden. "Gentlemen, we have guests. I believe you know the Gangers."

Hix got to his feet and came over to kiss Lenora on the cheek. "You are looking lovely."

Kel snorted. "Romeo, these books are heavy.

Move it."

Adrea patted the kitchen table. "Put them down here."

She asked for a larger space in the kitchen and a larger table, and everything started to shift.

Lenora and Harcourt stood together, and everyone watched as the space expanded, chairs grew up from the floor and the table widened to suit up to eight people.

"I will be back in a minute. Have a seat."

Everyone took positions around the table, and she went to get the herbs from the drying house.

She returned to her guests and felt a knock on her mental door. She opened the gate to Hyl. "Hyl is on his way in."

Hix nodded. "Good. Kel, put the water on to boil. I found the tea set."

She took her handfuls of herbs, rinsed them in the sink and then stuffed them into the huge pot. She poured the boiling water over them and wiped her hands dry.

"All right. You have some books for me to look at?"

Harcourt smiled. "This was a challenge. The Ritual Space information is hard to find. We asked our house to see what it could find, and these are all the results."

"Well, I am on a crash course here. We had better get started."

Harcourt pulled a book and opened it to a page with an image of the pyramids. "This book is in High Goblin."

Adrea took a look at it, and to her delight, the

words shifted and became something she could read.

The words *borrowed power* appeared multiple times on the page as it described the unfettered access to the ancient site without leaving home.

The next book was in the language of leaves. Elvish. It described the use of the new forest and dark forest for meditation and celebrations.

The next book was in another language, and the pages were written in blood.

The tomes they were handing her were huge histories. She looked at the pile, and a small, ragged, leather volume called to her.

She dimly knew that Hyl had returned, but she needed to learn more.

She stopped Harcourt when he would have handed her another large book, and she slipped the small book out of the stack where it had been pinned.

Adrea opened the book, and everyone in the room faded away.

She was floating in the air. Her feet didn't touch the ground. A woman in glowing robes with long white hair and piercing blue eyes approached.

"So, finally one of our line has bothered to seek the origins of our home."

Adrea swallowed. "I am not seeking the origin; I just need to understand."

"To understand, you must know where we came from."

"Who are you?"

"Darathrea, daughter of Athrea the knowing.

One of your ancestors."

Adrea absorbed that. "So, not a lot of variation on naming the girls, then."

"We needed a tie. The names were the easiest way."

"Well, how did it start?"

"My mother, mother of seven daughters, all with magic, was widowed in an area where mage craft was not desirable. She wanted her daughters to master their magic enough to hide it, so she created the ritual area where only the invited could come. Power was borrowed from ancient wonders and natural magical spaces. She mirrored it using simple enchantments that used her blood as a focus."

"So, she basically willed the space into existence?"

Darathrea snorted. "Of course not. She willed the magic into enhancing and assisting in hiding itself. That is the focus of this land, to let those with magic learn without judgment or persecution. It is a teaching space."

Adrea looked around. "Why do I feel something is missing?"

"Because you are perceptive. You have only begun to touch on the power of the land. I will show you how she came to create it and what she became in the process. You will know what is missing."

Adrea turned and watched a woman with long brown hair step into the water and spread her arms to the sky. She was weeping uncontrollably. The figure of a man rose out of the water, and she walked to him, never sinking into the waves. When she embraced him, they sank beneath the surface.

Silence ticked by, and the light of the scene moved from day to night to day again. The water frothed and a woman rose out of it, her bright-blue eyes visible, even from Adrea's vantage point.

She walked to the shore and fell to her knees, still weeping. The sky broke open, and it rained.

A line of little girls, the oldest a teenager, ran toward her. The girls were wearing black, and it made sense to Adrea. Ritual Space had been made to protect Athrea's daughters by surrendering completely to the elements. With her husband dead, the land became her protector.

"I think I understand. She got her power from opening herself to the land."

Darathrea smiled. "Precisely. She was grieving and made a choice that could have destroyed her, but it lifted her up. All curators of the property are given that choice, but no one has taken it. You will know it when it calls."

"Thank you."

"You are welcome. Consult the journal when you need guidance. I will be here."

Adrea blinked and saw several sets of eyes staring at her.

Harcourt frowned. "Aren't you going to read it?"

Hix smiled. "The tea is ready."

It seemed that no time had passed for those around her.

"I will pour."

She got to her feet and walked over to the teapot. She touched it, and it was still exceptionally hot. Her moment of revelation had been exactly that. A moment.

Her mind reeled, and she set the pot on the tray before bringing it over to the table. "Would anyone care for tea?"

Luning came through the door carrying a dizzying array of grocery bags. He greeted the Gangers and unpacked his haul on the counter before washing his hands and putting together a huge sub sandwich.

Adrea poured tea for those around the table, and when she sat, she asked Harcourt, "May I keep this journal for a few days?"

"Of course. If you can glean any information out of those scribbles, you are welcome to it."

She opened the book again, and he was right, her conscious mind couldn't make sense of the script, but the instinct told her it contained what she needed to work out what she was becoming or what she could become. She had the funny feeling she wasn't done yet.

"I am definitely getting something out of it."

Luning slid a wide chunk of sandwich in front of her before serving the others. "You need to eat."

Lenora smiled. "It is nice to have someone keeping an eye out for you."

Harcourt took his wife's hand and raised it to his lips. "It certainly is."

She ate with one hand while holding the books with the other.

The demons didn't have much to say aside from the fact that they couldn't break in, but an oracle mentioned the rise of chaos through the heart of magic.

"I think I have something." She looked up.

Everyone had their sandwich in their mouth, and she snickered at the image. She continued reading, and there were more mentions of rising chaos and the blood of the guardian.

"Well, if he was trying to open the gate by killing Neadra, it didn't work." She muttered it to herself.

Kel raised one perfect brow. "What?"

"There is mention of chaos being released with the blood of the guardian. If the killer intended to do it, it didn't work."

Luning scowled. "What if he tries again?"

She smiled tightly. "I won't be meditating."

He looked surprised for a moment before he smiled slowly. "You have some training?"

"Neadra brought in an instructor during the summers I spent with her. I have never had to use it, but I can defend myself against a physical attack if I have to."

The XIA agents looked sceptical, but Detective Luning looked at her with an assessing gaze. "Are you willing to prove it?"

She shrugged. "After a shower. Yes. I want to get into my own clothing before I do anything strenuous. I am not sure that Neadra's clothes are up for it."

Lenora smiled. "Go on. We will be here when you get back."

Adrea looked to Luning, and he nodded slightly. "I will be back in ten minutes."

The men had amusedly indulgent expressions, but Lenora grinned. "Go ahead, dear."

Adrea got up and headed to her room. The water of the shower revived her and someone had hung her clothing up in her closet. Her underwear was neatly arranged in the drawers, and she was desperately hoping that the house had put the clothing away and that it hadn't been the XIA agents or Luning.

With her own underwear on, she felt a little less vulnerable. The jeans and t-shirt clung to her like a second skin. She finally felt like herself again.

With cartoon socks and her favourite sneakers on her feet, she headed back downstairs.

Hix smiled. "Eight minutes, twenty-four seconds. Well done."

She made a face and went to find her phone. There was a message and a text. She put it on speaker while she read her text.

The funeral was set for dusk the following day. Mr. Grant's voice reiterated the information. She sent him a confirming text.

When she returned to the kitchen, everyone was checking their phones. Apparently, waiting for her to confirm the time was all that Mr. Grant's staff had been waiting for.

She sipped at her calming tea and listened to the conversations around her. They had gone through all the tomes and the light was reddening outside the windows. The study session had eaten most of the day.

Luning looked at her. "So, are you ready to prove you can defend yourself?"

She glanced around. "Not in here. The house might take exception to it. Let's head for the yard."

She took the journal and tucked it into the bookshelf in the living room. The house sealed it the moment she closed the glass case. No one was getting in there without her.

With her link to the past safe, she headed out the front door, leading a parade of folks who wanted to see what she could do.

She just hoped that performance anxiety wasn't going to kick in.

Chapter Eleven

There was no warning. Two arms wrapped around her and lifted her off the ground.

She kept herself calm and kicked back at her captor's knees and inner thighs, clawing at his hands with her short nails.

Adrea dropped to the ground as Hyl staggered, and on hands and knees, she kicked out at his jaw. He thudded back to the grass, and she quickly got to her feet.

He was much larger than she was and could easily carry or drag her, so standing was her best option.

He sat back and rubbed his jaw. "It seems you are prepared to defend yourself effectively."

Kel handed Hix a fiver.

Adrea felt outrage. "You bet against me? I thought elves were wise."

Hix snickered. "Not this one. He has been single for centuries for a reason. His ability to underestimate the fairer sex never fails."

Kel frowned and then shrugged in acknowledgement.

Adrea snickered. "Is there any of that sandwich

left?"

Lenora and Harcourt took their leave with the books, and she walked them to the transport area. Lenora sighed. "We will see you tomorrow to wish Neadra the best on her way to the next life."

To Adrea's surprise, Lenora dumped all of the books into Harcourt's arms, and she hugged her.

The last time Adrea had been hugged by a maternal figure, she had been three inches shorter and had broken her leg. The hug had come from a friend's mother while they waited in the emergency room for her parents to arrive. It had felt like the woman holding her wanted to protect her from the pain. That sweet feeling had stayed with her.

Blinking tears away, Adrea smiled when Lenora released her. "See you tomorrow, Lenora. You too, Harcourt."

He smiled sadly. "I deplore the circumstances, but I feel that you have some interesting things to offer to Ritual Space."

She chuckled as Lenora worked to open the portal with her cooperation. "I have nothing to offer but myself."

Lenora opened the portal and turned to say, "Most times, that is more than enough."

They stepped through and disappeared as the rift between spaces closed.

She sighed and turned to see the XIA agents approaching.

They grinned. "We have to make our reports and check in. Another team is pulling in right now. They will keep an eye out until we can get back here."

She missed them as soon as they headed for the gate, but she felt the polite chime in her mind that meant it was someone who had previous authorization to come and go at the property.

When the team arrived, Luning made the introductions. Benny, Smith, Argyle and Tremble all looked fresh and ready to do duty as security for her.

Adrea smiled. "It is nice to meet you, Benny. Your parents were just here."

The woman with rainbow eyes smiled. "I can feel them. I am sorry for your loss."

Adrea nodded. "Loss and gain seem to tangle together in my family."

"May I take a run around the property in a shifted form?"

Adrea gave him a look. She saw lion features overlaid Smith's. "Only if you do you not hunt. If there is one dead rabbit on my property, you will end up chained in the haunted forest."

He gave her a small salute and stripped down to the skin.

Adrea felt Luning come up behind her during the striptease that preceded the shift into an exceptionally large lion. Smith accepted a stroke and caress from Benny before he turned and took off into the darkness.

Adrea could sense the path that he took through her territory.

Benny grinned. "We are not here to keep you up. You go about your business, and we will keep an eye on you."

She looked to Benny and thought of that book.

"I do have something that I want to do."

Luning spoke to Benny, "I will stay with her."

The delicate, young woman who had dozens of extranormal races stamped on her aura inclined her head. "We will take care of everything out here."

Adrea nodded her thanks, but her mind was already back in the house and looking through that book. If her ancestor wanted to speak to her, she was ready to listen.

After spending the night speaking to her ancestor, she understood so much more about her family dynamic. The women who took over Ritual Space could not usually have children, though it did happen now and then. The inheritors and offspring were generally created before the women took over the space.

Eventually, Adrea got some sleep, and when she woke, she dressed for the funeral. It was nearly noon and the caterers would arrive soon.

As she left her room, she saw Luning in the shadows. "Please, tell me that you slept."

He stepped out of the shadows and smiled. "I did."

"What else can you do standing up?"

He grinned. "Do you want to have that conversation today?"

She blushed. "I... never mind."

She headed downstairs and wandered into the kitchen. She stared into the fridge trying to decide what she wanted.

Luning pushed her aside. "How did you survive

before you came here?"

She shrugged. "Takeout."

He made her another omelette and one for himself.

"So, are you ready for the events today?"

She got a chime in her mind, so she opened the gateway. "I am. I have figured out how to open the gates remotely, so I don't have to be there. I am horribly impressed with myself."

"How do you know who is coming through?"

"Whether I know them or not changes the timbre of the sound I hear." Adrea smiled and sighed at the feel of a full stomach again.

"And you hear it in your head?"

"Sort of. It translates into a noise I have heard before, and the journal told me that it is the way my mind has adapted to the link."

"The journal *told* you?"

She wrinkled her nose. "It's complicated."

She got to her feet to do the dishes when there was a knock on her door.

A quick check told her that Mr. Grant was at the door. "Excuse me, Hyl. My lawyer is here."

He chuckled, and she winced after being caught calling him anything other than his last name. She had been so good about calling him Luning. It was only in her thoughts that his actual name crept in.

She headed for the door and greeted Mr. Grant. "Good morning."

He smiled tightly. "Good afternoon. I have Gera here organizing the caterers and the event planners, but would you come out to expand the available space?"

She nodded. "Sure."

She walked out into the afternoon sun and stepped along with Mr. Grant. When they got to the area where the funeral would be held, she was a little shocked at the bustle of activity.

Immediately, she could see the problem that she had been called out for. The trees needed to be pulled back somehow.

"I will see what I can do. I am still new at this."

Mr. Grant beamed. "Of course."

It took a bit of focus and some convincing, but the trees bent and pulled their roots under the soil. It was either that or the ground rose to cover them, but when two hours had passed, she had enough seating for an extra hundred guests.

She stood and stared at the open gate and the stream of refrigerated boxes and heating units for the food. The caterers were a mix of species that was mindboggling. The colourations ran from chalk white to charcoal and every colour of the rainbow in between.

Mr. Grant was speaking with an older woman who looked a little goblinish and carried a clipboard. Gera was organizing the placements on the buffet table that took up forty feet of the large pavilion that had been erected.

To Adrea's eyes, this was a completely different place. She followed Mr. Grant's directions, and all too soon, she was getting ready for the funeral as dusk approached and the guests arrived.

Everyone was seated and waiting before she was asked to open the gateway for the funeral home. The procession was slow. Eight hooded

Ritual Space

men carried Neadra's body out of the portal, and at Mr. Grant's direction, Adrea followed behind.

To her surprise, her father and mother were sitting in the crowd as she followed her aunt's body to the pyre that had been set up for it.

The scent of daisies and irises followed her, and it was only when some of the guests pointed that she realized she was leaving a trail of her aunt's favourite flowers sprouting in their wake.

When her aunt was set in place, Adrea stood to the side and behind the pyre, waiting as the service began.

Luning remained in her peripheral vision, as he had throughout the day. Seeing his dark-clad form when she was wavering with thoughts of her aunt was comforting.

She was going to have to get used to the idea of life without him. Once they caught Neadra's killer, he would be out of her life.

The ceremony took half an hour, and the next hour and a half was spent with those who had met Neadra when she had taken over Ritual Space. There was a surprising amount of folks who had been coming to the property for centuries.

Finally, Adrea was asked to speak, and she stepped forward. "Um, first, I would like to thank everyone for coming. Neadra was the person I thought of when I wanted comfort and also the one I thought of when adventure was on my mind. She was kind, smart, no-nonsense and straightforward. If you wanted to know something, you simply had to ask. She would explain things as well as she could even if she didn't care for the subject matter."

Adrea chuckled. "Spending my summers here during puberty told me she would definitely answer anything."

Those gathered laughed.

"She also had the biggest heart when it came to helping those in need. I was in need as a child, and she took me in, teaching me and helping me grow. She mentioned leaving me something after she died, but I never imagined that it would be her hair colour."

More laughter rang in the air.

"I will miss her for what she added to my life and respect her for what she kept from me for my own good. Neadra Yoder, we will miss you."

Those gathered murmured, "We will miss you."

The man organizing the service walked forward with a torch, and Adrea took it.

"From fire to earth, you will be missed. And sorry about the outfit." She touched the torch to the pyre, and it caught fire.

The flames spread and crackled out around Neadra as the blaze increased.

The priest took the torch from her and nodded for her to step back. "We are all called upon to share our recollections of Neadra and enjoy the fellowship of a meal. Take as long as you need. The hospitality of the space has been extended to all of us."

Adrea nodded with a smile, and she watched the fire consume her aunt.

The entire space around her shuddered as Neadra disappeared into ash and smoke.

The guests left their seats and headed for the

tent. When Luning came to her side and pulled her away, she brushed at her cheeks to clear the tears and went to greet her parents.

Chapter Twelve

After she spoke with her parents, Luning asked, "So, they are made of ice?"

She chuckled. "No. Just hostility and greed. It is harder to thaw than ice."

Adrea stood in an open area so that anyone who wanted to could come up and hug her as well as talk about her great aunt. She was in one of the short lulls in the process.

The crescent moon was rising, and the nocturnal guests were waking completely.

Adrea faced another few hours of meeting strangers. Many of the guests simply came to make themselves known to her for the purpose of renting time in one of the environments.

When Mr. Grant made his way to her, she smiled and shook his hand.

He smiled. "I was surprised that she wanted to be burned."

Adrea blinked. "So was I. She wanted to be buried with the previous curators. This was a bit of a shock, but since you have all of her documents, I thought that it was in her will."

He scowled. "I was told it was what she had discussed with family."

She didn't have a chance to ask who had told him that. Someone shouted, "Fire!"

Adrea felt a burning on her forearm, and she ran out of the tent, flicked off her heels and sprinted through the crowd toward the flames licking the trees.

She wasn't sure about what she was doing, but she begged for rain.

The meditation house was engulfed in fire. Adrea halted, her feet throbbing from the run on uneven ground, and she watched the place where her aunt had died burn to the ground.

Tears flowed down her cheeks, and the rain came.

"You can't do anything else, Adrea." Benny and her team were there, and Luning was with them.

"Who would have done this?"

The fire was slowly fading, but the walls and ceilings were already destroyed. A building made of wood didn't stand up to flames.

Benny reached out and hugged her. "When her body was burned, it was done without safeguards. Her blood caught fire and that included this crime scene."

They were both soaked to the skin, and Adrea started shivering.

Luning came up and put his arm around her, pulling her away from Benny. "You need to get dry."

She fought her fury and looked at him with narrowed eyes. "Where is my father?"

Benny looked at her and cocked her head. "Why?"

"Because there is only one other family member that Mr. Grant would have consulted." Adrea lifted her head and sought the traces of her father.

"Either follow me or come with me, but I am going to have it out with him." She left him and began running.

The trees moved from her path, letting her run in a straight line to the spot in the dark forest that she had visited once before.

She could feel Luning behind her, but he was a few minutes away. The property wasn't powering him as it was her.

Adrea stopped and stared at her father, his suit rumpled and his expression uncomfortable.

"Why did you do it, Dad?" She walked further into the clearing.

He jumped, and his expression turned ugly. "This was mine. It was all for me. I was promised it until you arrived."

She stared at him. "Who promised it to you?"

"My mother. She said I would inherit."

"You never could have. If you didn't have a girl, Neadra would have found a way to have her own daughter. No male has ever had a place in command of this property and none ever could."

He lifted his hand, and he sneered. "With this vial, I can summon Apep, lord of chaos, and he will give me what I need."

"If that is Neadra's blood, I really wouldn't open that vial."

He sneered and looked to the spot in the grass where the pillar of smoke had appeared.

"You have no say in what I do or don't do. In a

moment, I will be in charge of Ritual Space and you will follow in Neadra's footsteps."

He opened the vial, and a cascade of flame shot out. He shouted and dropped the container. "What happened?"

She raised her brow. "You arranged for Neadra to be burned in Ritual Space. Contagion magic means that all of her body burned. Even her blood."

He looked shocked. "I need the blood of the guardian."

"And you killed Neadra for it? You are an idiot."

That was the wrong thing to say. He grabbed for a branch, and he struck at her. She dodged the first few strikes, kicking out at him, but then, she felt the impact on her temple and she was thrown onto the base of a tree.

Her father used the sharp end of the stick to pierce her wrist, and he cupped the blood in his hands, carrying it over to the portal before dumping it while he chanted.

Adrea muttered, "Our family can't do magic."

Her blood was seeping into the ground, and the pain in her head made it hard to think, but she saw arms covered in bark reaching for her, and she reached back.

The tree cradled her and lifted her high into the branches as she gave what was left of her life to the property and everything that lived on it.

Luning ran to the clearing in time to see Adrea's

father dumping blood on the ground.

The spiral of smoke that came up had the sinuous look of a serpent.

The trail of blood led to the trees, and it was dripping down the trunk.

Luning couldn't get up that tree, so he took on the opponent he could manage.

"Step away from that portal."

Adrea's father turned and snarled. "This is none of your business."

"You have assaulted your daughter. That is my business."

"She got in my way. I needed her blood."

Luning moved in and grabbed the man around the neck, pulled him off his feet and pinned him to the ground. "Where is Adrea?"

"What do I care?"

"She is your daughter."

"She was an accident."

"That doesn't matter. She is your blood."

The man in his grip twisted and struck at him. Luning shifted, and struck Mr. Morrigan in the head.

The column grew heavier. It hissed at him. "He could not deliver what I needed. I can make your dreams come true if you bring me the blood of the guardian."

The rustle of the canopy drew his attention, and Luning looked up to see Adrea descending with a vine around her waist.

Her eyes were glowing a violent blue, and her hair illuminated the woods. "Apep. You are not welcome here. I will tear you to pieces if you dare to creep through my soil again. This is your warning."

"I am not yours to command, curator."

Adrea grinned. "I am no longer the curator. I am Ritual Space."

Wind, fire, a tumble of earth and a jet of water came out of Adrea, and it wrapped around the god trying to crawl through the magical soil, and it shoved him back into the ground.

Luning looked at her in shock. "What is that?"

Adrea walked over and pressed a soft kiss to his lips that managed to electrify his entire body. "That is what we were meant to be, guardian. Haul him along, and we will see him punished for the murder of Neadra."

Luning flipped her father over and got his cuffs out of their case at the base of his spine. He wrenched the man's arms together while Adrea stared at the world around her with her glowing eyes.

Her gaze fixed on the direction where the mourners were still gathered. "He's still here."

Before Luning could react, she was moving through the woods in her tattered gown.

He hauled her father to his feet and dragged him behind her. Something was about to happen, and she might need backup.

Adrea felt truly alive for the first time in memory. Every nerve sang, and she knew every living thing in her territory.

She moved through the woods, and they touched her softly in greeting. When her body had completely recovered, she would not need to walk through the forests but rather be able to go where she was needed. That was a skill for another day.

Today, she needed to find the other soul anchoring the chaos spirit, and she needed to deal with it.

The mourners stared at her as she walked through the crowds. A quick glance told her that her dress was shredded and her arms and head were covered with blood.

Mr. Grant came toward her, but she held up a hand to keep him back. Her mother was speaking with Gera and that is where she headed.

"Hello, Mom. May I have a word with you?"

A crowd surrounded them as her mother slowly turned to face her. The poison green of her eyes burned in her pale features. "Adrea. What is it? You look horrible."

"I feel horrible. Can I have a hug?"

Her mother jerked in shock. "Why?"

"It is a funeral, Mom. Folks hug each other."

"You are all bloody."

"Yeah, well, it has been a freakish evening." She stepped toward her mother, and she cut her off when she tried to escape.

The hug began as a restraint, and it turned into a punishment as her mind sought out Apep, god of chaos, and she didn't just exorcise him, she shattered his corporeal contact.

When she looked up, a group of mages had surrounded them, and they were chanting and energy was humming to keep the god from escaping into another member of the gathering.

She kept going until she had routed every fleck of power that didn't belong to her mother out of her soul. All that was left was her animal, and when she was sure, she let her mother go.

Leanne Morrigan staggered back with a hand to her head. She looked around with wide eyes. "Where am I?"

Lenora Ganger stepped forward and took the woman's arm. "What do you last remember?"

"I... Adrea's birthday party."

Lenora looked to Adrea and kept speaking in a soothing tone. "How old was she?"

Leanne smiled. "She just turned five. Adrean asked me to sit with him in the back yard and have a cup of tea. It tasted funny, and I got sleepy."

Adrea blinked and stepped back, but she kept her mouth shut.

Leanne looked to Lenora. "Time has passed, hasn't it?"

Lenora nodded. "Yes, dear. You are going to have to go in to be examined. Magic was used on you without your consent."

"Oh. That makes sense. Is Adrea all right? She was going to Neadra's after the party. Is she with Neadra?"

Lenora put her arm around her and steered her to the outside of the crowd, speaking to her in low tones.

Benny and her team followed, and Adrea watched from fifty metres away as her mother was put into custody with the XIA team.

Luning brought her father out of the woods, but her mother had already left.

The gathering murmured in shock as her father kept shrieking, "She was mine to kill!"

He kept screaming as Luning hauled him out of the gates, and Adrea let them go.

She turned to the hundreds of folks who looked shocked by the events. "Please continue to share tales of Neadra. This evening marks the conclusion of her story. Celebrate her life. I will return in a moment."

Mr. Grant nodded cautiously as she passed him, and she headed back to the house in order to shower and change her clothing.

The evening gown on her bed was deep pewter. She took it as a hint, and when she had washed the blood from her skin, she dried off and slipped on the gown. The pewter chiffon flowed around her legs, and it was at that point that she realized she was not on the ground. Her steps carried her an inch above the solid surface, a warm column of air was under her feet.

The mirror showed her that the scars from the night had already healed. The pattern on her wrist wasn't a stab mark; it was a tree that ran up her inner arm. The mark on her temple was a spiral in a dark blue that stood out against her skin and hair.

Her horror of finding out that it was her own parents who killed her aunt was fading rapidly. Part of her had always known.

Now, it was time to speak to those who wanted to share stories of the previous curator, and Adrea wanted to listen.

Chapter Thirteen

Adrea was sitting next to the pile of ash that had been her aunt when Luning returned.

He sat next to her and took her hand.

She smiled. "He has been charged?"

"He has been charged. He has also been charged with inciting possession in your mother. She is in with the healers, trying to find her missing time."

"So, she wasn't really my mother for the last two decades." She nodded.

"That is what seems to be the case. She will need to catch up with her missing time, but her family is coming in to take charge of her. They will integrate her back into their gathering, and things will right themselves for her... eventually."

"Two parents in one night. That is a record in my family."

He nodded.

She looked down at his hand holding hers. "So, now that the mystery of the murder is solved, I suppose you will be resuming your duties?"

He chuckled. "I thought I would take some leave. This has been a little stressful for me, and I need some spell practice. A little more work on my part and I could have found the trail much earlier."

She nodded. "It sounds sensible. I am going to do some renovations here before I open fully for business."

"What kind of renovations?"

"I want a camp ground, and we obviously need a new meditation area."

He chuckled and squeezed her hand. "Camp ground?"

"Yeah, I talked to a few of the ladies, and they mentioned that they had been members of the Mage Guides and some of the men had been Scouts. Having them here would definitely give them a sense of what controlled magic can do in the world."

"I also noticed that you said *we*."

She scooted closer to him. "Well, there is no better place to practice magic than Ritual Space. I might need a little bit of security around here as well. When you get back to work, do you think I could get you on loan?"

He smiled. "I am sure that they would, but would you really mix business with pleasure?"

"Well, we seem to be able to separate them so far. I would suggest we give it a try." She bit her lip. "I do have to engage in full disclosure though."

He stroked her temple where the spiral stood out. "What?"

"You were what they were looking for. It wasn't my blood that would pull Apep through, it was yours. The blood of the guardian touched by death.

Apep was a death and chaos god. He needed your blood in your position as guardian to open the gate."

Luning scowled. "You didn't tell me that."

She wrinkled her nose. "I didn't know it was you until you came after me. At that point, I was being hauled up the tree to die."

"What?"

She cleared her throat. "I had to surrender myself to the space, and I had to do it before I was gone. The property rushed the transformation for time, but I will have to spend some time flexing my new wings, so to speak."

He slid his hand into her hair and turned her head toward him. "Are there actual wings involved?"

She smiled at him. "I don't think so, but there hasn't been an elemental here since the first days of Ritual Space. She was bound to the water, and I am trees and air."

"You learned that in the journal."

Adrea kissed him lightly and then leaned back. "It isn't so much a journal as a downloaded version of the daughter of the first elemental of Ritual Space. Everyone after has been a curator, until now."

"So, you don't really read it."

"Not really. When I said it speaks to me, it actually does. I have learned about the history of the area, the history of my family and why we kept the men out of controlling the space."

He brushed his lips against hers and whispered, "Why?"

"Our men are mages. They want to use the power. The women just look after it. We can't do anything when we step away from our property."

"So your father was a mage?"

"Untrained. It apparently made him a little crazy."

He pressed his forehead to hers. "Apparently."

They sat in silence, and the dawn began to creep up over the horizon.

She got to her feet and said, "One final thing."

She stepped onto the platform where her aunt's ashes were resting.

Adrea closed her eyes, raised her arms and a spiral of wind picked up the previous curator and swept her ashes into the air before travelling to the burial area and driving them into the ground. The column of swirling ashes continued to burrow into the ground until it was gone. A patch of irises and daisies bloomed on the spot.

Adrea walked—or floated—over to the burial site. Luning followed her but stayed back several feet.

"Auntie, I am so sorry that this happened to you. I never suspected that my father would take his obsession to this extent. I knew he wanted power, but I had no idea that he would kill to get it."

She sat next to the resting place and put her hand on the grave. "Know that Ritual Space is in good hands. I will keep it safe and continue to expand the property and the collection of magical places. I am going to be bringing children here to experience it, and I know how much you love children."

She wiped the tear that curled down her cheek. "It will be full of laughter again, as it was always intended to be."

A spectral cascade of laughter rang in her mind. Neadra was enjoying the plans for the future. She would remain here, in this place, until she wanted to leave. She was part of the property now and her ancestresses were with her.

Adrea spent some time sitting and listening to the laughter and singing. A rustle in the grasses told her she wasn't alone, and one by one, the bunnies came forward and put a fresh daisy on the bed of flowers.

She sat with her companions until the sun streamed in and lit the flowers. The bunnies scattered and played in the sunbeams. If Adrea focused, she could see Neadra walking in the woods beyond.

Sighing, she got to her feet, and she walked up to Luning. "So, you are on leave, you said?"

He offered her his arm. "Yes. May I ask a question?"

"Of course."

"Who told you about my history?"

She chuckled. "That is a mystery for another day. What do you want to do today?"

"I wouldn't mind a tour. Something on foot."

She linked her arm with his. "We can start with the light forest and work our way around to the lake."

"You don't mind that I was raised as an assassin?"

"We all have to start as something. I worked in

a teashop, and I would like to do something like that again, one day."

"Would you?"

"Yes. I liked helping people get through their days. I would mix up the herbs and send the client off to a mage to activate the spells."

"You really can't use magic?"

"Nope. Outside this place, I am powerless and surprisingly normal. Just one of the ten percent of humans without power in the world."

"Not anymore."

"Well, the human thing is now in doubt. I am still not used to walking around like this." She pointed at her feet.

"I like the added height. I don't have to fold myself in half to kiss you." He turned and demonstrated.

She felt him smiling against her lips as she rose up on a cushion of air until they were face to face. She braced her hands on his shoulders before slowly sinking back to stand beside him. "I like the new options."

"Are they comfortable? Do you feel different?"

"I feel healthy and like my skin is a little too tight. There is so much more to me now. More energy and ways I can use it."

They walked for an hour, stopping to pick fruit in the light forest. She greeted each tree as they passed and whispered to the brambles.

Luning watched her with an amused delight she wasn't used to seeing.

"Why are you laughing, Luning?"

"I think you can call me Hyl. I am not on duty,

after all."

"Fine. Hyl. Why the giggles?"

"I didn't realize that you spoke elvish."

She rubbed her nose. "I don't. This is the language of trees. Elvish uses more *th* sounds."

The trees laughed and whispered that they had taught the elves to speak, as the goblins were taught by the caverns and the trolls learned to talk from the stones.

She grinned.

Hyl smirked, "Now why are you grinning?"

"They are telling me that nature invented language and only the intelligent could pick up on it."

"I didn't hear anything."

She laughed for a solid five minutes.

He changed the subject. "What will happen if another wave dumps more magic into the world?"

"Ritual Space will remain the same. The purpose of the curator is stability. During a wave, all the power will rest inside me and emerge when it is safe."

"Will you change?"

"Probably not. The property might expand a little, but that has been the only side effect in the last few waves."

The trees whispered an offer to her. She paused. "If we could get around faster, would you be amenable?"

He shrugged. "Certainly."

She touched the shrubs and asked them for their help. The trees sprouted vines, and in fifteen minutes, they were looking at two bikes.

"You are kidding me."

She laughed. "Nope. They got the shape and function from my mind. The property is the power source."

He looked at her gown. "Can you even ride in that?"

"Of course. It doesn't have a heated motor, and it will balance itself. All we have to do is tell it where we want to go."

She walked over to the first bike and hiked up her skirt to straddle it. It was strange to feel it adjust to her as she settled.

"If I fall off, we are going to have words." Hyl growled it as he straddled his own cycle.

She leaned forward, and the cycle moved, gradually increasing the speed until her skirt was fluttering wildly and her hair was whipping around her head.

Hyl passed her, and she heard his joyful laughter as they sped on silent vehicles through the paths that opened up for them.

It was the start of a new era for Ritual Space, and her guardian finally joined the curator. If he behaved himself, Adrea might even tell Hyl one day. *If.*

Chapter Fourteen

Adrea stood in front of the wreck of the meditation house, and she cocked her head. A deep breath and she raised her hands, sending trees through the base of the house and ripping the charred hulk apart.

Hyl was off at the XIA headquarters giving a deposition. She had the whole place to herself.

It was time for a little renovation and reconstruction.

The wood cracked and popped as it was crushed by the living bands of trees.

She couldn't bear to have anything else on this segment of the property. It would eventually become a memorial garden, but for now, the forest would consume and cleanse the site of the violence that had changed everything.

The bunnies were supervising her as she wandered around looking for a proper site for the new meditation zone. Hyl had probably asked them to keep an eye on her. He was developing an affinity for the fluffy critters.

Adrea wandered around, and she spotted the area where they had held the funeral. It seemed

Ritual Space

perfect for her needs, so she paced out a five hundred-metre circle before dropping stones on her path.

She wasn't good at this part yet. She lined up north to south and clenched her fist, bending and making a bowling motion. A cascade of air parted the grass and left a long line through the soil.

Adrea exhaled a sigh of relief and moved to the east-west marker, repeating the gesture. She knelt and pressed her hand to the circle. The soil turned itself over and rocks rose to the surface in the marked area.

She spent hours carving designs into the ground and growing a canopy of trees to shade the centre as well as create seating.

When she was done, she sat in the new circle and looked around. Stones had risen onto all of her cut pathways, and the designs were rather pretty if she did say so herself.

The chime on her mind told her that she had finished in the nick of time.

She dusted off her jeans and got to her feet, opening the gateway while she walked to the portal.

Her entourage milled around her feet as she went to greet the Gangers.

Lenora came up and hugged her. "Adrea. You are looking very well."

Benny followed her mother and took her turn with a hug. "Power must agree with you."

Adrea grinned. "Power must because Hyl doesn't. I say I am ready to leave the property, and he insists that I need more time."

Benny smiled. "Take the time and get used to the new you. I speak from experience when I say it takes a bit of getting used to."

Adrea nodded. "Thanks. Well, ladies. Did you want to come in for some lemonade, or shall we scope locations?"

Benny rubbed her hands together. "Locations first?"

Adrea smiled. "Which ones?"

Lenora cocked her head. "Not to be indelicate, but the area where we held the funeral for Neadra was very nice and held everyone. What about that?"

Adrea nodded. "Definitely a possibility. Shall we?"

They walked away from the entry area, and Adrea tried a new trick. There was a light flash, and they were standing in the field.

Benny paused. "Whoa. That is different."

Adrea snickered. "Don't tell Hyl. He has no idea that I can do it. I just figured it out two days ago."

Lenora looked incredibly pleased. When Adrea followed her gaze, she saw she was staring at the new meditation zone.

"Perfect. It is absolutely perfect."

Benny sighed. "Shouldn't we at least look at some of the other environments?"

Lenora grabbed her daughter by the hand and hauled her to the zone. "Do you see this? Mage glyph, shifter glyph, vampire and elf. They are all here."

Adrea winced. She must have been thinking about it. "Sorry about that. I just thought they looked right."

Benny looked down and then up at her. "They are just right."

The mage sprinted toward her and hugged her again. Apparently, Benny had picked her spot for the full-moon bonding ceremony that was as close as she could get to a wedding.

Adrea had registered herself as a wedding official. It had taken an hour online, and it turned out that Ritual Space had a dispensation for weddings. All she had had to do was fill out the transfer of ownership paperwork that Mr. Grant sent to her.

Benny gave her another squeeze. "This is perfect."

She laughed. "I am glad you like it. It was one of my designated projects today."

Lenora chortled and rubbed her hands together. "Excellent. Now, I believe lemonade was mentioned."

They took a few steps and were on her front porch.

Lenora stumbled, and Adrea caught her. "Sorry. I should have warned you."

"No, no, it is fine. I am just not used to unannounced transports."

Benny helped her mom into the house while Adrea got the tray and lemonade with a plate of cookies.

Benny looked around and whistled. "This place has certainly gotten a makeover, even from last week."

Adrea shrugged. "I had to make room for Hyl, and he likes books. The house is now hosting about half of his collection. It makes for interesting and creepy reading late at night."

She set the tray down on the coffee table and poured tall and cool glasses of lemonade for each of them.

They sat and drank, discussed wedding details and the floral designs that Adrea was going to try and design the day of the wedding.

Benny paused. "I know Mom hasn't formally asked you, but would you perform the ceremony? The guys are worried about their alphas and makers fighting for the right to do the deed."

Adrea blinked. "Sure. I mean, I have done the online course and gotten certified by the state, so I can legally do it. Are you sure? I tend to run off at the mouth."

Lenora grinned. "You will be in good company."

Benny reached over and patted Adrea on the hand. "I will send you a format so that things can run smoothly. We will have your name printed on the programs and that will be finalized."

Lenora smiled and got a narrow piece of paper out of her purse. "Here is what it will look like."

Adrea looked, and under *Official,* it said, *Adrea Morrigan.*

"Well, thank goodness I said yes."

They grinned at each other and all grabbed cookies. It was a nice afternoon.

"And so, do you all swear to uphold the honour of your union, to defend your partnership and rejoice in the companionship you cement here today?"

Ritual Space

Benny stood slightly in front of but centrally with her three mates.

As one, they all said, "We do."

Under the glowing moon, the flowers on the shelter above them bloomed.

The crowd was surrounding them, all standing and waiting for the moment when Adrea announced, "I now pronounce you bonded mates in the eyes of these witnesses and the law. You may now kiss each other in whatever order you choose."

Benny laughed and was silenced as Andrew grabbed her for a kiss. Cairbre moved with the suddenness of the undead and grabbed their bride next. Gelendor waited his turn, but he bent her back completely to the astonishment of his family and the amusement of everyone else.

Benny's maid of honour handed her the bouquet when the formalities were done and the group was ready to head to their party.

Adrea sighed in relief, and flowers bloomed in front of the newlyweds as they walked to the reception tent.

Freddy turned and gave her a thumbs-up. "Great job, Adrea. I think you are going to be doing a ton of weddings."

Adrea's knees were weak as the most stressful event since she had first felt the stabbing in the teashop was over.

She followed the group at her own pace. Hyl walked up and supported her with an arm around her waist.

She was used to his touch now. When she woke screaming in the night, he held her until she calmed. Eventually, she would be over the fact that her father wanted to kill her and did—in fact—kill his own aunt for her blood and power. She could push the memories back when she was awake, but in the night, she depended on Hyl for comfort.

Catering staff were running ragged to bring food to the happy grouping and keep up with the guests at the buffet.

Adrea and Hyl sat at the outer edge of the gathering, and she kept the aura of peace on the group. This was a volatile situation that could explode if she let her guard down.

The Gangers had three hundred guests, and the vampires, were-lions and elves made up the rest of the reception. Wars had been fought with smaller quantities of people.

She remained on alert when one of the waiters brought her a plate and slid one in front of Hyl as well.

Adrea thanked him, and he blushed to the tip of his pointed goblin ears.

He ducked his head and scuttled back to the buffet.

"The food looks really good." Adrea took a bite and nodded. "It is really good."

Hyl forked up something from his own plate before he nodded. "It has to be or the clients would eat them."

She chuckled and started to relax.

The dancing was amazing. Some of the species seemed to have additional vertebrae that allowed them to bend in strange and unusual manners.

Ritual Space

There were formal and graceful dances, riotous songs that had the shifters and more obvious extranaturals thrashing around to the rhythm.

Adrea was standing near the edge of the gathering when a pale woman with dark hair came up and inclined her head. "My compliments for your excellent facility and your performance as official. Do you think you could officiate blood ceremonies?"

"Um, thank you. Adrea Morrigan." She extended her hand.

The pale woman blushed slightly. "Leonora Wicks. The mayor's aide. Sorry. I forget you are new to this environment."

"I am new to Redbird City. I have been living out of town for over six years."

"Right. Of course."

"To answer your question. Yes. I can definitely officiate at a blood ceremony. If you want to use the property for the day required, I can arrange a crypt in the dark forest."

Leonora beamed. "I will be in touch."

Adrea nodded. "I have a group of Mage Guides camping overnight this weekend, so we will arrange the time."

"Of course. The little ones have to practice somewhere."

Adrea could feel Leonora's energy, and it was confusing. "Pardon my rudeness, but are you a vampire?"

Leonora laughed. "I am not one to consider that rude. No. I am not. The technical term for me is apprentice or familiar. I am bound to Mathias, but he has responsibilities to me as well. It is an odd partnership."

"I would like to hear that story if you would like to tell it."

Leonora looked over to where the mayor was in deep discussion with the alpha of the lion clan. Adrea listened with rapt attention as the story unfolded.

She cried at one point, and a bank of mist rolled in. She quickly got herself under control, and Leo finished her story.

Adrea twisted her lips. "Can I write that down? Make a record of it?"

"Sure. I am supposed to, but I am way too lazy to bother with it. I always find other things to spend my time on."

Adrea grinned. "I always loved doing other people's homework. I will let you know when I have a rough draft and you can come and check it out."

Mathias came over and retrieved his assistant. He extended his hand to Adrea. "It is nice to meet you under more cheerful circumstances."

"I agree. I hope you are enjoying the view."

He looked down at Leo. "I am. Very much so."

Adrea blinked and watched as the mayor walked to the dance floor to dance with his assistant—and apparently—lover.

Hyl came back from his discussion with a group of XIA agents. "May I have this dance?"

She smiled and put her hand in his. "I thought you would never ask."

They swept to the dance floor and joined those

swaying slowly to the music.

It was the perfect end to the perfect day. It wasn't her wedding, but Adrea enjoyed that fact. Rushing into a permanent situation was not on her agenda. She had all the time in the world and enough space to call her own. *What more could a girl want?*

epilogue

The next wave of magic was coming. Adrea could feel it. The rabbits were avoiding exposure, and the weather was always a little bit off.

On a commercial level, Ritual Space was booming. Adrea's new greenhouse was producing herbs with built-in magic that could leave the property.

The amount of funds she was adding to her already-groaning coffers was incredible.

Writing Leo's story took up her time when she wasn't attending to the stream of clients that was coming in for access to the magical environment.

The call on her cell caught her by surprise. Hyl came onto the back porch with her phone in his hand. "Just a minute. Yeah, here she is."

"Hello?"

"Ms. Morrigan?"

"Yes."

"We have located a creature that has all the hallmarks of something that escaped from your property a few weeks ago. Will you take a look at it?"

She nodded. "Of course. When can you bring it?"

"We are in your parking lot. We need you to

come out here."

"I will be there in a moment."

She hung up and looked at Hyl. "Remember that creature that ran in front of the mages who arrested me way back?"

"I remember you mentioning it."

"Apparently, it is in the parking lot."

She wagged her brows at him. "Care to join me?"

"Like you could stop me."

She took his hand and stepped off the porch, ending up at the front gates. She opened the door and stepped out to see the XIA SUV with its payload of a trailer with an animal strapped to it.

She walked up to the huge, scaly lizard. "Aw, baby. What did they do to you?"

He looked at her with sad eyes and settled his head down. She touched his side, and her mind did what it had been doing lately; it dissected the spell.

Laughter spilled out of her. "He is harmless. Get him into Ritual Space, and I will be able to get him back to his original state."

The XIA officers didn't question her, didn't interrogate her; they simply unhitched the trailer and pulled it by hand through the wide section of gate that she opened.

It was weird to wield such power simply by owning a piece of land.

She closed the door behind the officers, leaving the man-door open.

She walked up to the creature that had the misfortune to be enchanted at the moment of Neadra's death. The men casting the spell had used a number of phallic elements, and one joker had decided to toss in Viagra. Instead of using a snake, one of the other improvisers had used his pet iguana, and the enlargement chant had taken up residence in the nearest walking animal.

The result was a very large lizard.

With a deep breath, she drained the magic from him. Herbs appeared on the trailer, smoke, a bit of inexplicable beef jerky and finally the pill that had twisted everything to the side.

The iguana looked at her with panic, and she scooped it up. "Hey, scooter. You are okay."

She turned to the XIA agents, and they all had phones in their hands, recording her actions.

"Does one of you guys know anyone who needs an iguana?"

They looked to each other and shook their heads. She wrinkled her nose. "Ask around. He isn't going to survive the winters here."

They looked a little less amused by that.

She held him as they removed the trailer and the incriminating ingredients.

Hyl looked at the lizard. "What are you going to name him?"

"Adolphus."

"Serious name."

She chuckled and headed back to the house. "You have no idea. She's a girl."

Adolphus looked at him primly and flicked her tongue.

"Wonderful. I am outnumbered."

She grinned. "Better you than me. This was a

lizard with a destiny, and now, she needs to plan for what happens next. I think I can help her with that."

Hyl smiled at her as he put his arm around her and they transported to the house, walking across the porch.

"Adolphus has taken well to sudden transports."

"She is a lizard of many talents. I am sure that a second destiny is just around the corner for her."

Hyl whispered in her ear. "You would know."

Adolphus gave her a look of complete agreement. Apparently, she would know.

Author's Note

I have decided to release Ritual Space on Jan 30th because it is my sister's birthday.

Six years ago, my sister and I discussed the basic plotline of this story for sixteen hours on a road trip. Since that day, she has asked me every six months if I had written the story yet.

When I created the Obscure Magic series, I knew that Ritual Space would fit right in.

The next book will either be *Defying Eternity* also known as Leonora Wicks's story, or *Binding Magic,* Minerva's story.

Thanks for reading,

Viola Grace

About the Author

Viola Grace (aka Zenina Masters) is a Canadian sci-fi/paranormal romance writer with ambitions to keep writing for the rest of her life. She specializes in short stories because the thrill of discovery, of all those firsts, is what keeps her writing.

An artist who enjoys a story that catches you up, whirls you around and sets you down with a smile on your face is all she endeavours to be. She prefers to leave the drama to those who are better suited to it, she always goes for the cheap laugh.

Made in the USA
Charleston, SC
28 May 2016